The Wolfe Tones
Phenomenon

Alex Fell

ISBN: 978-1-911131-34-2

This book was published in cooperation with
Choice Publishing, Drogheda, Co. Louth,
Republic of Ireland.
www.choicepublishing.ie

The Wolfe Tones Phenomenon

Cover: Alex Fell [Derek photograph: Caroline Tan] all photographs Alex Fell except where stated.

The Balladeer Cuala Press.
In 1898, Jack B Yeats visited the grave of Theobold Wolfe Tone The
Bodenstown Churchyard, political leader of the United Irishmen, and
thereafter his art subjects were exclusively of Ireland.

Acknowledgements

The thing about the Wolfe Tones is the pure joy of their concerts. Singing along at the top of your voice with lyrical ballads and rousing choruses, the feeling of solidarity and listening to heart rending stories keeps everyone coming back time and again and it is this that is so hard to convey when faced with the responsibility of doing justice to a complex story.

I wish to thank all members of The Wolfe Tones past and present for each in their own way creating my ideal working conditions for facing a big challenge. There were no expectations or influences put on me whatsoever. I was however given access to the archive photos by Derek for which I am extremely grateful, as I am sure will be members of all their families in years to come. I am also very grateful to Martin Dardis for his generosity in giving me free access to his website. At the outset a comprehensive history was not anticipated but it was essential to slot The Wolfe Tones into their place in the developing story of Ireland. A story not for the faint hearted.

Such monumental international success by any standard as musicians and chroniclers of Irish history could not be allowed to be disappeared by politicians for whatever reason. Draconian measures have been successful to the point of me encountering, even now years later, ignorant but well formed prejudices which it is hoped will erode with the passage of time. Delight on the other hand is expressed by the people who actually go to the concerts and think for themselves. It is hoped they will enjoy a permanent record of a band that lives and records with the courage of their convictions and is truly the object of global affection. It is probably true too that they are the world's best ballad band and all the hundreds of thousands who go to see them repeatedly know it.

Alex Fell
August 2017
County Cork [The "rebel" county!]

Contents

Foreword

Let me be quite clear, it is not possible for a band to be much more successful than the Wolfe Tones in the things that all band members value: chart success, consistently packed venues for years, the keys of cities, platinum CDs, and public accolades for quality. At the same time, it is not possible for a band to be more misunderstood.

It is no secret that the Wolfe Tones is a wonderful band. No secret, that is, to those in the know who happen to be folk-music lovers, Irish patriots, and those who care about Ireland. This includes the worldwide Irish diaspora, whom they have reminded of Ireland for fifty-four years at the time of writing. To everybody else, they are a mystery and an undiscovered delight. Hard work and outstanding musicality has achieved a level of excellence that has not only gained them worldwide success but enabled them to represent the Irish internationally.

They have been playing together for so long that they have witnessed various political changes, and through no fault of their own became caught up not only in an internecine propaganda war but also in the strange views that various governments held about a united Ireland and the steps taken to prevent it from happening. Or not? That is the question: one of many, including issues of public order and anger management, and including the power of song. Central, is the legacy of the bloody history of Ireland over eight hundred years that dare not speak its name.

Essential questions are raised, such as the implication that Irish people are volatile, unstable and easily influenced, even to the point of violence. That the use of the legal process is justified to gag opposing views, including even songs, and that the majority of the electorate are not worth listening to. Why is this? Could it be that Ireland is too weak economically to survive without trade with UK, so dare not cause offence? Have Irish governments colluded in the social control via the legal process that Britain exercised for more than eight hundred years, on and off, by force?

Undoubtedly, all governments have an obligation to protect the lives of their citizens, but must they, like poor children, be discouraged from asking for the impossible, for fear of destroying the country's ability to afford basic essential services, and eventually perhaps social policies on a par with those of the UK? This may, realistically, be the main reason so many in the North want to remain part of UK. Services such as the National Health Service, 'free at the point of delivery', and taxation rates. In other words, is it merely that the timing might be premature and so must end in bloody and expensive failure, harming the ability of the country to unite eventually by economic and legal means through negotiation?

On the other hand, individual politicians may just have been too scared of being the ones who permitted the re-ignition of the terrible bloodshed of the civil war of the 1920s. The irony is that by putting effort into suppressing the influence of the Wolfe Tones, and other bands, they may in fact have enhanced it, and so, without going out of their way, the band may have become the poster boys for those who want a united Ireland – something which was calculated to be the majority of the law abiding electorate. And the others too, perhaps?

Meanwhile, The Wolfe Tones has not only been denied the so-called oxygen of publicity but have been subject to concerted attack by those who should know better, even suffering too dissension within the band itself, resulting in stress, conflict and the threat of legal tangles. Despite this, they have remained true to their roots, their integrity and their beliefs, achieving significant worldwide success. History will show that they have performed an important function in Ireland's evolving 'struggle for freedom' by involving the diaspora. Not, as scapegoated, by inciting violence within Ireland, but by encouraging world support, enabling the diplomatic assistance from America leading to the Good Friday Agreement of 1998 and paving the way to the readmission of Northern Ireland to the EU after Brexit. And all through the power of traditional and original music and song!

Chapter 1

The Band Now

The Wolfe Tones have been together, at the time of writing, for fifty-four years – longer than the Beatles and about the same as the Rolling Stones, suggesting hard graft, strong bonds and leadership, effective commercial strategy and consistent entertainment. In this time, they have experienced the greatest success as a consequence: everything a band can experience in terms of highs and lows, and then some.

The band was started by Brian Warfield and Noel Nagle, and Brian's brother Derek; later Liam Courtney joined them, and was subsequently replaced by Tommy Byrne. They were also joined for a time by Phillip Woodnut, Derek's fellow musician from another band. Now everything is reduced and distilled in all senses with the departure of Derek after thirty-seven years, as a result of serious friction. The lineup, from left to right on stage, is Brian Warfield, the dynamic force of the band; Tommy Byrne, considered Ireland's finest ballad singer; and Noel Nagle, who, as a talented traditional tin-whistle player, is responsible for the key Irishness of the sound that opens the door to the Irish diaspora.

Looking at the empty stage while the venue fills, one is struck by the precision of the arrangement of the equipment. Nothing has been left to chance; the only thing missing is guide chalkmarks on the stage. Somebody, Cecil Carter perhaps, working with Dwyer McClorey, the business manager, has eyes with built-in tape measures. Most noticeable is the area on the extreme right around Noel's stool, which is laid out like the cockpit of an aircraft or an operating theatre – which, in effect, it is. On its own is a laptop, which he supervises, for the PowerPoint projection on the back wall. Beside it is his armoury of tin whistles. No gazing into space for him.

When the band discreetly appear, the wild applause and cheering is spontaneous, unlimited and completely unsolicited. They are immaculately and modestly turned out. They don't speak, they don't smile, and as they wait to be counted in, they are, for all the world, like professional orchestral musicians watching the conductor. This should not be surprising because that is what they are and this is what they do, but it *is* remarkable, given their huge reputation and the tendency of popular music to go for the hard sell. Perhaps some of the fun has been dissipated by implied criticism over the years. They certainly have nothing to prove.

What most other bands do not have to deal with, however, is political controversy and victimization, and the ignoring of their greatest achievements, which would earn others titles (such as Bob Dylan's Nobel Prize), and recognition of their contribution to the national economy. They have withstood this like the Fastnet Rock amidst the storms and crashing waves, and have still kept going. Along the way, they have been caught in the crossfire of internecine propaganda and been criticised, but not necessarily harmed, despite concerted efforts by interested parties. An example of this was the complaint from a politician from Ulster about a historical song they had recorded being played on a plane to America, 'A Nation Once Again', written by Thomas Osborne Davis in the 1840s, which had been voted the best single of all time in a BBC World Service poll. Even this monumental achievement had been denigrated as being the result of enthusiasm by the Irish diaspora. All entertainment industry votes are the result of enthusiasm, and the Wolfe Tones were the focus. They truly are one of Ireland's most popular folk and ballad bands worldwide.

Perhaps the absence of fun is in part because of the need not to add fuel to fire by being overtly partisan. In fact, the only discernible messages expressed in Brian's songs are compassion and the desire for peace, out of implied but identifiable Christian principles.

Then they start to play. What a transformation. With the first song, impressions are changed dramatically by the richness and musicality of the sound, which belies the conservatism of their appearance and is unequivocally Irish. Most striking is the perfect intonation, which means that you can relax and enjoy the concert, knowing that there will not be any discordant shocks. Something that one expects from professional musicians, but which is by no means always forthcoming.

The sound is presently created by Brian on the five-string banjo and vocals, Tommy on guitar and vocals, and Noel on tin whistle and vocals. At other times, Brian plays the harp and *bhodrán*, but he particularly enjoys the creation of the arrangements of the songs, many of which he wrote. They are assisted occasionally by Siobhan, Brian's daughter, with women's songs and accordion, and by Kiev Connolly on keyboards and additional guitar. He is seen on stage from time to time, as well as working behind the scenes with the arrangements, orchestration and coordination of orchestral musicians on high days and holidays.

"54 years on the road and still entertaining. As Brian once said "I wrote the song, "Let the People Sing" back in the sixties and I'd no idea that it was to become such an anthem over time.....Irish song has many facets to it, it was never sectarian. Wolfe Tone, Robert Emmet, Henry Joy, all Protestants, the story of Ireland is in the song lore of Ireland so nobody can make accusations of sectarianism against its content."

On tour, to ensure delivery of the recorded sound, they are accompanied by a soundtrack to augment the live instruments. Derek's departure left them short of a mandolin, although the banjo in Brian's hands shows its versatility, sounding at different times like a bass guitar, American Confederate folk and South American acoustic, and covers the featured riffs and chords in the songs concerned. Given the care that has gone into the arrangements, augmentation is entirely understandable, because every element again has been constructed so that the instruments individually fill the sound spectrum, not just from start to finish but in depth from top to bottom. The recorded sound, re-created live, is at times like the soundtrack to a film in terms of its skill in establishing atmosphere and context 'Lough Sheelin Eviction' and 'Child of Destiny'. The folk roots represented have stringed instruments more frequently plucked than strummed, each with their own melodic line. All harmonies are evenly balanced, so that no one is drowned out. When they sing in unison, they can sound both like a male voice choir, as on 'Newgrange', and the marching men of a flying column, in 'Come Out You Black and Tans'. One can almost see the razor and comb in the breast pocket and feel the republican itch. But it's all art! Like TV soap stars in supermarkets, identities can get confused. Even with just one note, the voices are instantly and deeply melodious. Everyone comes in when intended, not a fraction too soon or too late. Precision is all.

Anticipating live performance of all this would stop most people from thinking of anything else – which explains the flat facial expressions. It would wipe the smile off anyone's face. During the performance, there is a complete absence of vanity. No attempt to ingratiate with the audience, and no hard sell. No winking and smiling; no propaganda; just a tightly planned, closely rehearsed and perfectly executed programme.

Unusually for the music industry, each band member is in their own way a virtuoso performer. This recalls thoughts, not for the last time, of the crème de la crème of the classical world, the Berlin Philharmonic Orchestra, in which all the members are virtuoso performers selected by the orchestra members themselves.

The programme the Wolfe Tones perform has not changed radically over the years, being added to as they record new songs. The hits are always required, but there is also an enormous back catalogue to draw on for different audiences. Songs are available about the various parts of Ireland: 'The Green Glens of Antrim', 'The Cliffs of Moher', 'Newgrange'. Unusually, they play in a wide variety of musical genres and tempos, miraculously creating different authentic configurations of sound. This is an Irish tradition for which the touring showbands were particularly accomplished in the 1960s, having to entertain all the generations in a concert. The work involved in creating all this is immeasurable, not forgetting the constant modification of the artwork, photographs and portraits of the cultural history in the PowerPoint presentation, which is in synch with the individual songs. Another of Brian's accomplishments.

Significantly, they still sing the same historical songs that they performed in the beginning, when they were young boys, but as the political landscape has changed over the years, some of them have become more controversial. They sing other people's songs as well, of the different historical eras, like other Irish musicians who have not suffered the same opprobrium, or enjoyed the same success. Quite possibly, events may show that it is the very success of the Wolfe Tones that has drawn attention to them, and the feared but unproven political influence on their audience, that has resulted in the legally enforced caution of the national broadcasters. This secrecy may well have been counterproductive, however, and their notoriety the best unique selling point. Own goal for censorship! Despite it, they will be remembered long after their censors for their musically uplifting concerts.

The international venues they have visited regularly are largely linked to the Irish diaspora. We read of the success of the emigrants but perhaps forget that the present population of Ireland is descended from the survivors of tremendous hardship, and has learned from them. This is reflected in the workload of the Wolfe Tones over the years.

One thing is for sure: their entertainment value and musicianship cannot be faulted. Any comment must therefore concern the content of the songs.

Chapter 2

The Warfields

It all started so innocently back in 1963 in Inchicore in the Warfield family, where music was an important part of family life. Somehow all the brothers – Brian, and Derek the eldest, as well as Bernard and Noel – had acquired not just a love and appreciation of Irish music and song but the ability to play it and for Brian and Derek to perform it and go on to write it. This is remarkable in itself, but both also have outstanding business acumen: a highly unusual combination of skills. Brian developed an enduring love of Irish history, as well as compassion and a heightened sense of injustice. Derek, too, additionally researching songs not just in Ireland but of the Irish in America in historical events, has a political perspective on injustice and Irish character.

Inchicore is a working-class area of Dublin; the Warfield family have Scottish Irish influences. Their maternal grandmother lived in Hamilton, Glasgow, for a number of years, and their uncle Pearse was born there. Refusing to 'fire a shot for England', Paddy and Anne Cunningham returned to Dublin in 1915. Here is a clue as to where the boys developed their passion for Irish history, and the achievements of the Irish in their countries of destination. The grandparents made return visits to Glasgow with their daughter Olive and received very warm welcomes, so naturally Glasgow holds a very dear place in all their hearts. For Derek, it was a particular pleasure to sit with his grandmother and listen to her reminiscences of Glasgow Celtic Football Club, which he had supported since his youth. One of his football match companions was Luke Kelly of the Dubliners, and even Tommy on occasion. He well remembers going with Luke to the team's matches, and the excitement surrounding the team's victory in the European Cup in 1967. When he talks about the pleasure of going to matches, it comes as a shock to discover that they actually played at the stadium as part of the 'Celtic Celebration', during which Glasgow Celtic played the Republic of Ireland in a testimonial for the manager, Mick McCarthy.

Ireland v Celtic testimonial weekend souvenir (Wolfe Tones Archive)

The Wolfe Tones play regularly in Glasgow, a favourite venue being Barrowlands Ballroom, with great affection all round but latterly amid some controversy. Unsurprisingly, they all support Glasgow Celtic Football Club. Mr Peter McLean, the club's public relations manager, said: "It is always important to distinguish between the right to one's own cultural ideas and bigotry', referring to a complaint he said the 'Wolfe Tones wrote back assuring us they actively worked against sectarianism throughout the world, and were fiercely opposed to it,' 'Celtic is proud of its joint Scottish and Irish identity, and is keen to retain it. Unfortunately, some people cannot distinguish between culture and bigotry." The Celtic People expands on the

Wolfe Tones' point of view.

The Barrowlands experience is one they all always speak of with wonder because of the enthusiasm of the audience; so does everybody else who is ever present. As Derek recalls 'In 1988, Michael Hand travelled with us to Britain and we performed at Barrowlands, Glasgow, and The National, Kilburn.' In an article he wrote for the Sunday Independent, he described the crowd

> "You ain't seen nothing yet" concert at the Barrowlands 'and in the case of our own Wolfe Tones appearing at the Barrowlands there are some 50 to 60 policemen sweating under the strain of bringing some semblance of order to eager young men and women clutching green scarfs buff tickets squeezing towards the entrance. There is no agro, just a heave or two to get out of the cold and into the hall; buses lined up outside from Newcastle, Dumfries and Aberdeen disgorge their passengers onto cold wet streets. The police bear the pressure of the crush. And within 20 minutes more than 3,000 fans gain admission. There was a rapturous reception for the Tones and they belt into "The Boys of the Old Brigade", the teeming swaying throng cheer every word. 'Some say the Devil is dead,' sings Derek Warfield, and the floorboards groan with stamping feet, and so it goes. The Wolfe Tones know their audience, and more importantly the audience knows them."

Derek, the eldest of the four children, was born in Inchicore too, in 1943. He was educated at Synge Street CBS and was later apprenticed as a tailor, only to find the lure of a musical career irresistible. His mother had encouraged him to sing, and taught him songs, which he enjoyed singing whenever he could. So much so that he made his first stage appearance at the age of six at the Queen's Theatre Dublin. His paternal grandmother, Catherine McDonough Warfield, gave him a mandolin when he was eight, and his father taught him to play it.

Derek differs in his form of passion for Irish history, focusing on the Irish diaspora – particularly the Irish who fought for America – and the songs commemorating their part in the events of the American Civil War, and the Americas in general. He wrote about the founder of the Argentinian navy, Admiral William Brown, coincidentally at the time of the Falklands War. This actually dated from a boyhood interest in Argentina, when he was set an essay task for homework about a place of his choice. Much later, he was seduced by a historic photo of an Argentinian hurling team in Ireland. His pursuit of American song was blamed for a rift in the band after thirty-seven years of playing together, and ultimately his departure from the group.

Brian was born in the Holy See Maternity Hospital, Dublin on 2 April 1947, the second of the four boys. At the time, the family lived in a one-roomed flat on the South Circular Road, and moved to a new house in Bluebell when he was seven. He attended St Kevins Junior School, then the Oblates School, Inchicore, and then went to St James's Christian Brotherhood School. The atmosphere at home was very musical, with both parents playing the piano and singing; their father also played the mandolin, which he would later teach to Derek. Their mother used to play and sing in the afternoons. Brian would later write the song 'Irish Eyes', dedicated to her. As he said, 'I can never remember a time without music or song in the house. In the Dublin of the 1950s, there was no television, just the wireless. The variety of musical knowledge we got was from those programmes, from classical to light opera, from Hollywood to Irish song and dance. My early influences in music were the ordinary people and my family, and the songs I heard on the radio. My favourite song was 'The Black Hills of

Dakota' and my favourite singer was Doris Day; my best-loved Irish singer at the time was Brendan O'Dowda.'

From the age of twelve, he was to learn the five-string banjo, the guitar, and the tin whistle with Noel. He is also a highly proficient harper (as they are called in Ireland). The two of them have recorded delightful traditional music for harp and tin whistle on Wolfe Tones CDs, including 'Carolan's Favourite' and 'Newgrange', Derek's beautiful neo-traditional song, demonstrating their authentic folk roots, as well as their musicianship. Brian also recorded some other harp music of Carolan the blind harper, 'Carolan's Concerto'. Harp music does not get more difficult or more Irish than that, unless you listen to Reels. This makes the distraction of the so called political influence on the audience all the more disrespectfully dismissive.

Brian, Noel and Derek schoolboy friends (Warfield Family archive)

Their futures were mapped out at an early age by the influence of their families, and by their regular attendance at their local traditional music club, Comhaltas Ceoltiri Eireann, effectively serving as an apprenticeship. This organisation exists to promote all aspects of Irish culture: song, dance, music and language. It also organises the annual Fleadh Cheoil festivals, including the proficiency competitions that were so formative for the Wolfe Tones.

Harry Warfield his sons,Tommy and Noel at Derek's wedding 1965Left to right Noel W.,Brian, Harry, Derek, Bernard, Tommy and Noel N.

Brian has written over two hundred songs, at least half of which have been recorded by the Wolfe Tones. He composed music for an Irish radio production of Shakespeare's *As You Like It* and a suite of music called *Exodus*, referring to what he calls the Irish Holocaust, the Great Famine. He has written songs that follow the traditional Irish ballad subject-matter of aspects of Irish life over the centuries, and document current events worthy of being remembered. His songs have been very successful, and recordings of those of others include two No.1s In the Irish charts and platinum CDs.

Wolfe Tones Trio

Noel with Brian, here playing the harp, in Philadelphia

His prodigious output is reminiscent of someone who, when asked the secret of their luck, replied, 'the harder I work, the luckier I get'. He is completely committed to Irish culture – the music and the history – and while touring with the Wolfe Tones may well have had in mind the travels of O'Carolan and the role of the balladeers in times past, especially Zozimus the Dublin balladeer, real name Michael Moran, who came from the Liberties, another working-class area of Dublin, as did Tommy – and the famous Robert Emmet 'Anne Devlin of the Hills'. His passion is recording the history of Ireland in music and song. This includes one of Zozimus's ballads, 'The Finding of Moses', sung by Derek. Unexpectedly funny, this must have influenced the honing of Brian's piercing wit in the writing of such songs as 'The Helicopter Song', Ireland's fastest-selling single ever (in pre-download days), and 'You'll Never Beat the Irish'.

Derek has had considerable success since leaving the band, including being commissioned to write and record a CD for the Australian National Folk Festival. He also released a number of CDs with his band the Young Wolfe Tones, performing songs the Irish took abroad with them when they were forced to emigrate. His proudest moment was being invited to perform at the White House for St Patrick's Day 2015 just before the end of President Obama's term of office and is also very proud of his award winning CD *"Washington's Irish"*

Derek and the Young Wolfe Tones at the White House St. Patrick's Day 2015 with Barack Obama The President of the United States of America and Enda Kenny the Taoiseach of the Republic of Ireland (Young Wolfe Tones archive)

Chapter 3

The Folk Music Revival and Noel

The harp music and song of O'Carolan, the blind harper of the eighteenth century, was collated and restored by Sean O'Riada, the Cork music lecturer and composer who is credited with initiating the Irish folk-music revival in the 1960s. At that time, most folk music was in English, which O'Riada passed over in favour of Irish music and song. He was also involved with the national radio of RTÉ, so may have been instrumental in commissioning music by Brian for the Shakespeare production of *As You Like It*. As part of his enthusiasm for Irish culture and language, he worked at the Abbey Theatre in Dublin; for one of the productions, he recruited traditional musicians, whom he rehearsed in order to unify their style. They went on to become the internationally famous Chieftains. He was influential on Noel's musical development too, as well as many other musicians.

Subsequently, the Clancy Brothers with Tommy Makem entertained theatregoers as part of their quest to become actors in America. They captured the attention of Pete Seeger and Woody Guthrie, stars of the American folk scene, leading to their recognition, and then the search for songs in Ireland. This was in the late 1960s. They were joined in the USA by Eddie Furey and the Dubliners, and the Wolfe Tones started touring in America to entertain the enormous Irish-American population eager for the sounds of their forefathers, which continues to this day.

On the Statten Island ferry (Wolfe Tones archive)

But of course the story of folk music is as old as the hills. Music is a very powerful means of communication common to all cultures, and is played in a variety of ways and at all important occasions, with instruments of varying levels of sophistication. The rhythm is as important as the sound, and together both are quite geographically distinctive.

The Celts brought music to Ireland from Iron Age Gaul, which covered most of France, including modern-day Brittany and some of Spain. It was played on the traditional instruments of *uilleann* pipes, fiddle, harp, Irish flute, tin whistle and *bodhrán*. The music was not written but taught by ear, logically, being about sound, and featured musical ornaments that were the speciality of the individual player, in the same way that composers feature grace notes, trills and mordants. This continues today with regional variations, such as the Sligo fiddle style. This is a huge topic for many separate studies. Suffice to say that, starting from the age of twelve, Brian achieved a high level of musical proficiency as a result of his family's passion for Irish culture and the frequent playing of the music on a windup record-player at home. He went to tin-whistle classes with Paddy Bawn O'Brin in Church Street, Dublin, where, in company with Noel Nagle and Finbar Furey, they learnt even more traditional tunes.

Noel Nagle, like Brian, was from a highly musical family. As he said:

> 'My father was the first big musical influence in my life. He taught pipes and drums, and had a very successful band called New Eire Girls Pipe Band. I began playing the guitar first, then moved on to the banjo, until I finally settled on the tin whistle. I also played the *uilleann* pipes, and a great pipe-player, Dan O'Dowd, made my first practice set for me. I was born in Dublin and grew up in Drimnagh. In the early 1950s we had to move to Bluebell, another Dublin suburb, to accommodate our big family of twelve children. I went to school in St Michael's Christian Brothers School in Inchicore. It was here that I first learned and became interested in the history of Ireland, and it was the Christian Brothers who first instilled the love of Irish music and rebel songs into me. The gymnasium at the school was where the 1916 leaders were brought after their arrest, and spent their first night of detention there, before being taken to nearby Kilmainham Jail, where they were later executed for their part in the rising.' (Martin Dardis) [bibliog].

As part of a large family, Noel and their friends used to play and sing together in the evenings and at family occasions, and, later on, after visits to the pub. With Brian they developed their love of traditional and historical Irish songs and music, and both were influenced by Noel's sister Marie's boyfriend,

Four nice young men looking inexperienced

Same nice young men transformed for a publicity shot by the influence of manager Oliver Barry

Tony Butler, whose record collection introduced them to the music of the Clancy Brothers and the American folk singers Pete Seeger and Woody Guthrie – although they did not know at that time that they would go to America as performers themselves.

Tony introduced them to the *fleadh cheoils*, or open-air Irish culture and music festivals, the inspiration and forerunner of the rock festivals; they were introduced to the songs and styles of the performers of the day, as well as enjoying time away from Dublin, travelling around Ireland. The first *fleadh* they went to was at Miltown Malbay in County Clare as an extension of the family get-togethers. In short, they had the perfect apprenticeship to the life of successful travelling musicians, and all the time they had been learning and developing their repertoire of traditional Irish songs. They had also had the opportunity to improve their musical technique, constantly being able to hear, and compare themselves to, the best Irish performers.

Noel & Brian - Early TV stills (wolfetonesofficialsite.com/wolfetonestv)

They started performing with some friends at local concerts in August 1963. This went well, and in October that year the two of them went to England and played at folk clubs managing to get residencies at four of them.

The Wolfe Tones - the era of the suits

After this, Brian and Noel joined up with Liam Courtney and they became the Wolfe Tone Group, while Derek returned to England there not being sufficient work for all of them. The trio were performing at Puck Fair in Killorglin, County Kerry, when they were approached by a Canadian television crew, who asked them to sing a couple of songs. When they were asked their name, they thought quickly, and came up with the Wolfe Tones. They had chosen the name 'Wolfe Tones', a play on words describing both a discordant sound on a violin and the Protestant patriot who nearly got the French to liberate Ireland from the British with some ships down in west Cork in the eighteenth century. Unfortunately, the ships were sunk in Bantry Bay. This led to a film session in Dublin. For the next few years, the boys played around the country in pubs and festivals for 'beer money'. Eventually, they all quit their jobs and headed to England to take part in the English folk revival of the early 1960s.

The following year, Derek and Philip Woodnut (from Bluebell), who were playing together in a group in Ireland known as the

Circle Group, came to London to join them. When they heard of the folk revival in Ireland, they returned that Easter; while at a fleadh in Roscommon, they met Tommy Byrne in McDermott's pub in Elphin. When they arrived back in Dublin, groups like the Dubliners and the Clancy Brothers were making waves across the entertainment scene. They started to attract mainstream attention and appear on TV and radio.

Around this time, they were joined permanently by Tommy Byrne, and released their first record, The Spanish Lady. Early publicity shots of the band show them in suits –looking more like the Beatles than Irish folk singers, it is said – but that was the style of the day. They also often appeared dressed in waistcoats at that time.

Things were difficult in the early days: they released several singles, none of which sold very well. They dabbled in Irish folk ballads, and American folk and rebel songs. Their first breakthrough came when their recording of 'James Connolly' broke into the Irish charts, eventually reaching number 15.

Derek had joined them in August, and the four of them had started to appear regularly on Ballad Session, a TV ballad programme. Around this time, they acquired their first manager, Kaare Jonson, a Norwegian. Pivotal events followed: they won the Rose of Tralee Ballad Group competition with 'Boston Rose'; they were discovered by Leslie Mann, the scout for Fontana Records; and Liam Courtney was replaced by Tommy Byrne, who had played with them from time to time, and had kept in touch with them. A recording contract followed in November. This was followed by their first album, at Phillips Studios in Marble Arch, London, known for being the studio where Wayne Fontana and his Mind Benders, and The Pretty Things had been recorded. As a result, they had many bookings on RTÉ TV and radio the following year, and regular appearances on the three weekend nights at the Four Courts Hotel, Dublin. These events were very successful, attracting guest appearances by other artists. In 1965 they worked on Mondays at the Old Sheiling Hotel, run by Bill Fuller.

Noel is a meticulous man – as you would guess from looking at the layout of his space on stage. Looking at his tin whistles laid out like operating instruments, it may come as a surprise to the uninitiated to discover that he has several of them, and not just the one that goes in the back pocket of his jeans or in his belt. This casual attitude is part of the mythology of the instrument. Many times a whistle player appears on TV and produces the instrument from the jacket inside pocket, and plays away. Actually, Noel does not wear jeans, and his several tin whistles are treated with enormous respect. Again this is a reminder, if it were needed, that the band are serious professional musicians and never were Saturday-night pub dilettantes. The fact is that the whistle itself has certain constraints, like the small number of holes, which limits the range and tone. Consequently, the size and length of the instrument is crucial to the pitch and tone of the sound which is produced. Add to this, the size of the bore and the resonance of the metal of which the whistle is made are both of crucial importance, as is the addition of accidental dents and damage.

It is all very reminiscent of the Clint Eastwood film *For A Few Dollars More*, about competing bounty-hunters tracking down bandits. The other one, played by Lee Van Cleef, is immaculate in black from head to foot, with a magnificent black horse. He steps out of the saloon just as a bandit is galloping like hell to get out of town fast. The bounty-hunter slowly and deliberately pulls a string on the rolled-up blanket on his saddle, which unrolls swiftly, revealing a collection of carefully stored and calibrated guns. Selecting a shotgun, he takes careful aim, as the bandit is about to disappear out of sight, fires, and stops him dead in his tracks. Cool, efficient and utterly professional! The truth is, however, that if the bounty-hunter were to attempt to compete seriously with Noel for efficiency, he would need Wells Fargo to transport his guns, because Noel actually has four sets of them which he uses in rotation. Given the touring schedule of the Wolfe Tones, this makes sense, and gives new meaning to the expression 'One on, one off, and one in the wash'.

Noel is pivotal to the band's success. His mastery of his instrument is quintessentially Irish: the sound is instantly recognisable as Irish and traditional, a primary pre requisite for appearing in America and the rest of the world for the homesick. The tin whistle is actually the last of the traditional instruments which has habitually been played by the Wolfe Tones and its history goes back to the Book of Leinster in the eleventh century.

Noel's intonation is perfect, irrespective of whatever is going on – which is not just reassuring, but a profound pleasure. The tin whistles vary in tone and pitch and have specific jobs, although they are all used at times to double Tommy's melodic line. His introductions to iconic songs are wonderful, with his characteristic trills and grace notes, which ornament without oppressing or irritating, giving total authenticity. Who can forget his introduction to the most recent recording of 'The Foggy Dew', with the mellow tone of the larger Chieftain low-F tin whistle. He seems to have affection for the smaller one with the blue mouthpiece – the Generation D – which sounds a bit like a recorder and was played on 'Mullingar Fleadh' in the early days. Then there is the one in the middle range with the extended mouthpiece that was chosen for 'Hibernia' and again the small Shaw nickel narrowing-bore one, or sometimes the Walton's brass one with a green mouthpiece, both of which Noel plays on 'Grace'. As with woodwind instruments, the final factor after the selection of the instrument, and in this case its key, is the professionalism of the sound created by the mouth and lips or embouchure. Adjustment to the intonation can be made by pulling out and pushing in the joints when they are present, such as the black Dixon with the prominent joint that makes tuning possible for playing 'Joe McDonnell'.

This is when the Berlin Philharmonic comes to mind again when James Galway, the Northern Irish flautist, impressed the other musicians so much at their extensive audition process. Galway had started out in his youth playing the tin whistle, progressing to the flute as an orchestral instrument. He is renowned for having a flute specially cast in silver to get the optimal tone; one can't help but wonder if the tinny sound he wanted to improve on just compared badly with a Chieftain low F in his own and Noel's hands.

In the balmy days before national politics got in the way, and the recorded songs became more defiantly political, Noel and Brian were recorded with Brian playing the harp and Noel playing a Chieftain low whistle (F?), as in the photograph of them in Philadelphia, playing O'Carolan's music perhaps or 'Newgrange', celebrating the ancient Celtic civilisation at the site that predates Stonehenge by 2000 years. His expertise is prominent on 'The Valley of Knocknurane', and the Zozimus song 'Finding Moses', both on *Up the Rebels*.

Chieftain Low F – The Foggy Dew

Dixon Tuneable whistle for Joe Mc Donnell and Sean South [he sings this one]

Mullingar Fleadh

Generation D (wolfetonesofficialsite.com) blue mouthpiece

The pipers grip – note his left hand with fingers further over whistle

Light a Penny Candle and Hibernia

Grace

Clarke: small metal narrowing bore, Shaw: brass with green mouthpiece, both play Grace also Broad Black Brimmer

Chapter 4

Ballads and Tommy

To many, a ballad is a sentimental song about love between two people. This is only part of the truth, however, and has come about because of the way the term has been used in recent years. The traditional meaning of 'ballad' includes this, but, more widely, refers to an account of something socially important, and follows an ancient tradition for spreading news or commemorating a significant event. In other words, ballads relate culturally important information. Hitler set out to destroy the recorded culture of the Jews, and in the Middle East ancient religious artifacts are also being destroyed. This is because these things, like the ballads, represent the sum of cultural experience, and the memory and formative experiences of a community.

Ireland's violent past has included the repression of song, and ballads specifically, because this was the means of the communication of ideas, information, tales of heroism and mockery. Dangerous stuff. It was considered subversive with severe penalties, of death or transportation. Captain Bligh, of mutiny fame, even had Anne Devlin's 'Anne Devlin of the Hills' cousin transported to Van Dieman's Land (Tasmania) for that, amongst other things.

The Wolfe Tones, rightly or wrongly, have become synonymous with 'rebel songs' – a dangerous term, because it has been used to label the singers as subversive similarly in some sense. The songs tell stories of heroic acts and historical events in the struggle to free the country from colonialism. In other words, patriotism.

Derek explained his view comprehensively: 'The way I always looked at the so-called rebel songs, the patriotic ballads, was that they were how the ordinary people of Ireland recorded their feelings and emotions. I always felt comfortable singing them because I grew up with them. I was just surprised when people didn't sing them. . . . Patriotic ballads are a huge part of our popular song tradition and deserve artistic merit. For many generations, it was the only means that people had to express their feelings. It was a response, of course, to English oppression in this country. Song has been a very powerful part of our resistance down through the years. People undermined its value and censored its sentiments; when these were songs that were sung in the GPO in 1916.'

Warfield quotes James Connolly: 'No revolutionary movement is complete without its poetical expression. . . . Until the movement is marked by the joyous, defiant singing of revolutionary songs, it lacks one of the most distinctive marks of a popular revolutionary movement, it is the dogma of a few, and not the faith of the multitude. . . . Everything in the nineteenth century was geared to denationalise the country. The songs then became part of that resistance. To me, the songs about the events of the Troubles, internment and the hunger strikers, they're just as important as 'The Ballad of James Connolly'. It was the ordinary man's response to the awful treatment of this country.'

In the same interview (*www.theirishrevolution.ie*), with Marjorie Brennan, he echoed the same opinion as Mark O'Brien (*Political Censorship and Democracy*), only applying it to song, not violence: 'Everybody looks for scapegoats in troubled times. The songs are not the problem; the songs are a response to the problem. This was our way to respond to our oppression.'

With music, it all becomes memorable. Modern teaching methods include singing the alphabet, for example; when more than two people sing together, a movement can start. National anthems can develop from such beginnings.

There are a number of types of traditional ballad subject matter of interest to the Wolfe Tones. These include ballads about Ireland as a country – historically a dangerous song topic, so often disguised in the past with a woman's name like Kathleen O'Houlihan and Dark Rosaleen – and about places in Ireland 'My Green Valleys', 'Green Glens of Antrim', 'Dingle Bay'; emigration 'Botany Bay', 'Flow Liffey Waters', the latter featuring a beautiful vocal with lovely mandolin accompaniment); famous people 'Padraic Pearse', 'Michael Collins'; love; terrible events and loss 'Lough Sheelin Eviction'; rebellion and civil war experiences 'Sean South of Garryowen'; and homesickness 'Flight of Earls'. Actually, they are all about love in its many manifestations.

Strictly speaking, all the Wolfe Tones songs are therefore ballads. Brian writes many of them, believing passionately that Irish history should not be forgotten or sanitised by neglect. The less savoury aspects are glossed over, like the Ballyseedy massacre described in Dorothy McCardle's *Tragedies of Kerry*, and the religious persecution of Catholics in England does not get a priority mention because he is, after all, a showman.

He can only do so much even in more than two hundred songs: the audience literally do not have enough time. No time for English Catholics like Guy Fawkes, who did his best to blow up Parliament in the interests of Catholic liberation – not when a three-hour programme is already packed with favourite hits. They might if he wrote a catchy song about it, like he wrote about the English monarchs, telling the Irish truth in 'You'll

Never Beat the Irish'. Catholicism, it should be made clear, is never singled out for mention. The songs written are in the interests of Irish humanity. In fact, the point is made more than once that religious division has been used by the oppressor to divide and rule.

Brian Warfield is actually a genius: the word is used correctly and soberly. A school comprehension test consisted of a description of genius as being like a volcano sharing the same roots as the land around, in the fire of the earth's core, but it alone having the ability to express it. We all share the ability to feel the same emotions, but only a genius can translate it into a form we can recognise and feel.

Brian also has the talent to write, in this case, ballads indistinguishable from traditional songs 'Foggy Misty Dew' and at the same time in a variety of musical styles 'Connaught Rangers' and inventive arrangements that both intrigue and resonate simultaneously. At his most reassuring and 'rebellious', he mocks frightening figures in his lyrics in exactly the same way a comforting parent tells a worried child to imagine the teacher on the lavatory. "Over in the Dáil they were drinking gin and brandy. The Minister for Justice was soaking up the sun". 'The Helicopter Song' unlike many great composers his work is unpredictable and richly varied. Hardly dangerous?

The Irish ballads in the modern sense are often described as lilting, which is about the tempo, not to be confused with the lilting Celtic singing of people like Bobby Gardner, which could be described as mouth music, imitating step-dancing sounds. This is a feature which can explain their popularity for physical reasons, being the rhythm of the human pulse, unlike rock music the tempo of which is roughly twice that of the heartbeat. It is resonant with the body, and conducive and resonant with the great human emotions of love and loss in the lyrics. There is too a musical resonance with lyrical expressive phrases. The songs are in essence about emotion.

Brian the Musician

This is why Tommy Byrne has rightly been described as Ireland's greatest ballad singer. Sometimes it is 'Ireland's greatest living ballad singer', out of respect for the late Luke Kelly of the Dubliners and his fans. Actually, there is no disrespect because they cannot be compared, having two entirely different singing styles, Luke Kelly having the sweet musical gravelly tone associated not just with the Dubliners but with quintessential folk music. Derek and Brian also come into this category.

Tommy is a different kettle of fish entirely, following in the great line of Irish tenor royalty Josef Locke and John McCormack. This is not an accident.
As he explained in an interview:

"Born and reared in the Liberties in the 1940s and 1950s, and the eldest of eleven children, I bought my first guitar in 1962 and taught myself to play. My early influences were Joan Baez and the Clancy Brothers, who were making it big in the US at the time, and I fell in love with folk music Irish and American.

Wolfe Tones in Killarney with Luke Kelly (Wolfe Tones archive)

By 1966 there were at least 800 ballad groups [in Ireland] and the folk boom had really taken hold. I began performing in the various folk clubs in Dublin and at the fleadhs around the countryside. It was at a fleadh in Elphin, County Roscommon, on Easter weekend, 1964 that I first met Brian Warfield and Noel Nagle, who were members of a ballad group called the Wolfe Tones. We played and sang together all weekend, and within the year I had left my job in the Guinness brewery and joined the band full time, and, thank God, I have never looked back!

Early TV still (wolfetonesofficialsite.com/wolfetonestv)

There is so much more to say about Tommy's singing that his modesty omits. For a start, no one with any feeling for music, or ballads, or Irish pride, can possibly be unaware of John McCormack, the international opera singer and concert tenor. Coming from the Liberties too, a working-class area of Dublin, John McCormack was not just an Irish hero and a musical god but a local hero. In 1918, when living in New York, he paid $75,000 in tax alone. The style is unfashionable today for light entertainment because you hear the voice training before the melody: to modern ears, it sounds a bit pompous. As a child, he sang in the local Pro-Cathedral choir, the Palestrino Boys Choir, which is known and respected internationally. Tommy could never be oblivious of this and for someone tuned in had to have heard if not participated himself acquiring the superb diction. For a fleeting moment at a concert, Tommy had the demeanour of a much-praised child, standing on a chair to sing for his relatives. His facial expression does not follow the modern fashion for acting the words, but everything is there in the inflexions of his voice. He would have listened many times to McCormack's recordings, even if he didn't realise it, in the search for songs at the very least and being in the same room as a radio playing his singing. To this day, barely a mile from where Tommy grew up, there is a singing school in the area that embodies the principles of John McCormack's professional singing style, bel canto of the Italian school; this has helped international singing stars of all genres cope with voice-strain and general technique. Oh, and outside the local church, St Catherine's, is a memorial to Robert Emmet on the spot where he was executed!

Between 1912 and his retirement in 1923, McCormack toured extensively. He was known not only for 'It's a Long Way to Tipperary', amongst many others, but also for the fact that he was able to sing sixty-four notes on one breath, as he did in 'Il mio tesoro' (Commendatore) from Mozart's *Don Giovanni*. This is worth listening to on YouTube. He was also on the radio regularly. So, interestingly, despite being, as they say, 'up to their necks in the muck and bullets' of the rebellion, it was not considered necessary to stop him broadcasting, even though he was known for supporting the movement for Home Rule, recording 'The Wearing of the Green'! He may, of course, have been out of the country, as he spent so much time in America. He died in Dublin, at Booterstown, in 1945.

Fundamentally, the style is about phrasing and following the expression and flow of the natural speaking voice, so that nothing is forced. Tommy has clearly been influenced by this style. Put this with the lilting rhythm in time with the pulse and the subject matter of emotions experienced physically, and you have Tommy's style in a nutshell. There are aspects, though, that are inherent, like the melodious tone and perfect intonation. He sings the difficult songs amidst complex arrangements, and yet hits the first note full on without wavering, and he has complete control in the long, naturally expressed phrases, so that he can express the subtle nuances of emotion, not just from time to time but consistently and with finesse. This gives his performances their sincerity, and adds authenticity to the words.

Given the subject matter of the songs, he finds the truth where others would just repeat pub songs. Technically highly proficient and consistent, he makes sustained phrasing and difficult intervals sound easy, and his extreme sensitivity offers subtle gradations and complete control.

Additionally, however, the Wolfe Tones sing in unison in a variety of styles: the tough men together in the choruses of 'The Boys of the Old Brigade' and the pure monk-like singing in Derek's 'Newgrange'. Tommy does another of Derek's songs, 'The Sailor St Brendan', so well, although apparently not keen to do it initially. Syncopated throughout, it cannot have been easy, but it sounds ethereal and joyful. Derek wrote it in 1984 to commemorate the 1500th anniversary of the saint's birth.

'The Cliffs of Moher', 'Boston Rose', 'Child of Destiny' and 'First of May' all express different aspects of human emotion at a level which is impossible to put into words, taking the lyrics to a new dimension. 'The Cliffs of Moher', by Brian, is about fleeting love, but also the nostalgia for the romantic visitor and missed opportunities, and as a DVD is a nostalgic travelogue for Ireland. 'Boston Rose' relates to the Rose of Tralee worldwide beauty and personality contest beloved of the diaspora; Brian's 'Child of Destiny' is about hope for the future expressed through the hopes for a child against the negativity of war, with fleeting impressions invoked by the arrangement. 'First of May', written and as recorded by the Bee Gees, passes unnoticed although commercially successful but the Wolfe Tones version makes you google the meaning and cuts you to the quick – well, it does if you are an animal lover!

What is easy to overlook is Tommy's guitar-playing. While he claims never to have practised, this cannot apply to the guitar. Jimi Hendrix, who drove everyone mad playing day and night to achieve his reputation, comes to mind. Tommy's is a different style, but is highly proficient. A video on YouTube of Tommy in a pub accompanying himself singing 'Streets of New York' is very telling, because it is a stand alone rendition. It is well known that art takes further the technical aspects of science, as anyone listening to early violin-playing trying to master 'Three Blind Mice' can testify.

Musically this is all very satisfying, and makes his contribution central to the success of the Wolfe Tones, but it would not be possible without the exquisite and varied songs that Brian writes for him. Brian has been quoted as saying how much he enjoys writing for Tommy. The miracle is that he still has his wonderful voice, given the demands of the tours. These go on for hours at a time, night after night, for weeks on end, on the band's regular tours all over the world, seeking out the Irish diaspora. Given the sentimentality of the lyrics and the vaulting melodic lines, the songs are unbeatable. Not a dry eye in the house. The songs with the rousing choruses, on the other hand, deliver the folk equivalent of stadium rock, and a message of encouragement.

It is my belief that the pitch of this type of voice has a particular popularity, I am thinking here of Josef Locke, because women can sing along with the words, and the pace of the lilting ballad allows time for the listener to remember the words: all part of the pleasure of participation. This is something which is recognised and encouraged by the Wolfe Tones.

For a self-effacing man, working with the Wolfe Tones has to be the dream job, with a personal songwriter giving him the opportunity to record beautiful traditional songs, such as 'The Water Is Wide', and exquisite ballads in the old style, like 'Misty Foggy Dew', as well as those with modern resonance, such as the folk ballads of the future also written by Brian, such as 'Joe McDonnell'. How wonderful for Brian to hear the definitive version of his songs night after night. A pity that the CD inserts make no reference to Tommy, or for that matter Noel, or their immense talents at all, their names being lost in the small print.

There is the paradox of stardom versus anonymity. Tommy must have had numerous offers to do other things, so his loyalty to the Wolfe Tones has to be deliberate. Being denied mainstream stardom by the knock-on effect of the propaganda war after the onset of the Troubles in the North, a disaster for those who have to rely on publicity and stagecraft to compensate for a lesser talent, may well have been something of a relief to Tommy. Despite this, to those hundreds of thousands around the world who actually go to the concerts, he is in effect truly an international star, purely on the basis of his outstanding ability. There is no doubt that he is in his element when he is singing the ballads. Every time, it is fresh and true; he comes alive then. He knows that the applause is merited. Those who hear him believe him to be the finest ballad singer in Ireland; many comments on YouTube endorse this.

Child of Destiny

Lonely Banna Strand

Cliffs of Moher

In 1966, the Wolfe Tones released their second recording on Fontana, '*Up The Rebels*', which was recorded at Eamonn Andrews Studio, Henry Street, Dublin. Also that year, the Wolfe Tones opened the Embankment in Tallaght on Thursdays for Mick McCarthy. In August that year, they toured America for the first time.

The following year, they employed a new manager, Oliver Barry. This was a successful arrangement that lasted until Oliver's departure to start Century Radio in 1988.
It really has been a remarkable career.

As Tommy said:
Since then we have performed the world a few times over, and in some of the most prestigious venues around the world, including Carnegie Hall, New York, the Royal Albert Hall London – and I must mention the Apollo, Glasgow, the most memorable gig of my life. We have played about forty states in the US, Australia, and all over the UK and Ireland, and played alongside artists like John Denver, Kris Kristofferson, Glen Campbell, Joan Baez and Status Quo.

Carnegie Hall Ticket (Wolfe Tones archive)

Tommy was there when they were given the keys to New York and Los Angeles. He sang at Carnegie Hall, the Paris Olympia and the Royal Albert Hall. It is his voice, with Brian Derek and Noel singing Ireland's fastest-selling single of all time. 'The Helicopter Song', and also when they were voted the best balland band at the Rose of Tralee festival, his voice singing the song voted in December 2002 by listeners to the BBC World Service as the best single of all time, 'A Nation Once Again', and of course there were the months in the Irish charts after going to no. 1 with 'Streets of New York' and 'Admiral William Brown' which went to no. 4.

It all puts you in mind of the great George Best once his football-playing career was over. A hotel porter walked into his bedroom and found him and a former Miss World with thousands of pounds thrown onto the bed. The porter said: 'Oh George, where did it all go wrong?'

Performance at the Paris Olympia (Wolfe Tones Archive)

Wolfe Tones with the Mayor of Limerick (Wolfe Tones Archive)

~ 45 ~

Chapter 5

1167

Daniel Maclise (1806-1870) The Marriage of Strongbow and Aoife, c.1854
(Presented Sir Richard Wallace, 1879. National Gallery of Ireland Collection
Photo© National Gallery of Ireland

In times of mass illiteracy, with only word of mouth for communication, the balladeers performed an invaluable function as a source of news and current events, and as travelling entertainers. However, back in the mists of time, sometimes this could be dangerous.

In Ireland after 1167 this is a masterpiece of understatement, because of censorship and social control. As the guide at the National Gallery of Ireland in Dublin said as she extended a hand expansively towards the large painting of *The Marriage of Strongbow and Aoife* by Daniel Maclise in the first room: 'The saddest day in Irish history!' What she meant was that the invasion by Strongbow (the grandson of William the Conqueror), otherwise known as Richard de Clare or the Earl of Pembroke, and his men, was the first colonisation of Ireland, and brought the British to Irish soil – along with repression, plunder, disease and starvation. And, for good measure, emigration to the four corners of the earth for millions of people for the next eight hundred years. She omitted to mention the Vikings, followed by the Celts, who had done something similar centuries before, but with more beneficial effect. Irreverently, perhaps, I find the painting hilarious. Weddings juxtapose curiosity about the family of the new partner with family pride, and the painting shows both. Aoife's obvious reluctance is how you would imagine a shotgun wedding. It is a marvelous painting but perhaps historically inaccurate. Correction: very inaccurate – not the least of the detail being that the wedding took place in a cathedral in Dublin.

For a start, the guide did not mention that Dermot McMurrough, King of Leinster and father of Aoife, had actually asked Strongbow to come to Ireland to help him regain his lands and kingdom from the King of Breffni, Tiernan O'Rourke, whose wife he had kidnapped in 1153. O'Rourke formed an alliance with Rory O'Connor, who was High King of Ireland. In 1166 this feud resulted in MacMurrough being driven into exile by the Gaelic chieftains. He fled to France. As an incentive he offered the hand in marriage of Aoife – which meant the inheritance of Leinster. The French influence was confined to the Dublin area, 'the Pale', for a long time, until, by inheritance, the monarch of England – by then King John, he who 'lost his crown in the Wash', and was forced to sign Magna Carta – added it to his kingdom. So Dermot willingly permitted the foreigner to rule eventually.

Prior to this, the country was composed of kingdoms and chiefs with a court bard who was a walking encyclopaedia of information, such as the lineage of the chiefs, important events and history. They were high-status because they could effectively make people immortal by reputation. The arrival of the French disrupted this.

The most infamous repressive legislation enacted in Ireland in subsequent centuries were the Penal Laws of 1695, designed to restrict the influence of the Pope and to force Catholics to convert to Protestantism after the Reformation. The Pope's role at this time was highly political, and affected all of Europe. To prevent his influence on the Irish via his choice of bishops, Irish Catholics were deprived of every aspect of citizenship, and any means of achieving status by Catholic education, influence through membership of a profession, trade or civic responsibility, prosperity earned or inherited, family life as recorded in parish records, vicarious or temporary parenthood, property ownership of any value, and ownership of land. Irish music and song was also banned. This amounted to cultural genocide worthy of Hitler, in fact. England was subject to these laws too. A sinister feature was the banning of jury trial for Catholics and the payment of informers.

After the defeat of the Jacobites in 1692 and the Treaty of Limerick, the bards emigrated, adapted or disappeared. According to Brian, England persecuted them, not permitting them to describe themselves or even dress as bards, only recognising the bards of Wales and Cornwall, themselves Celts. Poynings Law and the Statutes of Kilkenny reinforced this. The statutes begin by recognising that the English settlers had been influenced by Irish culture and customs, as quoted above. They forbade intermarriage between the native Irish and the native English, the English fostering of Irish children, the English adoption of Irish children, and the use of Irish names and dress. Those English colonists who did not know how to speak English were required to learn the language (on pain of losing their land and belongings), along with many other English customs. The Irish pastimes of 'hockie' and 'coiting' were to be dropped, and pursuits such as archery and lancing to be taken up, so that the English colonists would be more able to defend against Irish and foreign aggression, using English military tactics. Poynings Law required all Irish laws to be ratified by Westminster.

The English in Ireland had to be governed by English common law, instead of the Irish Brehon Law. The separation of the Irish and English churches was ensured by requiring that 'no Irishman . . . be admitted into any cathedral or collegiate church . . . amongst the English of the land'. In other words, a policy of deliberate colonisation, not integration, was pursued.

Statute XV forbade Irish minstrels or storytellers from coming to English areas, guarding against 'the Irish agents who come amongst the English, spy out the secrets, plans, and policies of the English, whereby great evils have often resulted'. Spying was the big fear of the age. Successive monarchs were equally repressive, and major events abroad were triggered by Catholic repression such as the Spanish Armada and the plot to replace Queen Elizabeth with Mary Queen of Scots. Even when they were banished to Connacht under the Penal Laws, bards were forbidden from taking their instruments with them.

The Balladeer Cuala Press. Alex Fell
An aqua tinted print from a woodcut designed by Jack B Yeats for his
sisters 'Arts and crafts' business.

The Balladeer Cuala Press.
In 1898, Jack B Yeats visited the grave of Theobold Wolfe Tone The
Bodenstown Churchyard, political leader of the United Irishmen, and
thereafter his art subjects were exclusively of Ireland.

Frank Harte, a respected singer, said: 'Those in power write the history, while those who suffer write the songs.' Distinctions have to be made between the purposes of the modern political songs. Some just observe, some raise awareness, and some encourage action. This is crucial to an appreciation of the role of the Wolfe Tones' songs. It is argued that none of them encourage action. Furthermore, some have an additional therapeutic purpose of providing support through solidarity between people. According to Wikipedia, until recently, rebel songs tell 'stories of real people fighting in the cause of violent republicanism'. This is an inaccurate and offensive definition, fortunately now amended, because violence is not essential to either the activity or the song. It is at the core of the controversy surrounding the Wolfe Tones, carrying automatic censure as a result of the private agendas of people desperate to maintain the status quo of colonialism. Even so, who would be the rebel in the Siege of Wexford scenario? Well, actually, no one, because the term was not used until the eighteenth century. Coincidentally, the American War of Independence took place between 1775 and 1783, so there is an association; the term 'rebel songs' could even be American, and taken up by the British. Attitudes in America are different – eased by the passage of time, perhaps. Certainly no one has a problem in talking about rebel yells, for example. Having said all that, it is a sad fact that colonial occupiers the world over invariably have to be made uncomfortable to relinquish control unless the administration is costly and inconvenient being half way round the world with a difficult language to master. Ireland is just too close and convenient to Britain.

On TV genealogical programmes, celebrities are delighted to discover a relative who was actively involved in the American War of Independence and the Civil War, never mind which side of the struggle. Wikipedia is not always accurate, and so-called rebel songs do not always advocate violence. Many are redolent with sadness 'Grace', 'Anne Devlin of the Hills', while others express a desire for peace 'Ireland Unfree'. Far from being subversive, Wolfe Tones songs may even support a Christian message, as in the Glasgow Celtic song 'The Celtic People'. So this labelling is a serious error, and its casual use has had fundamental consequences, but in America it may have even been coined as a useful marketing tool and then spread across the world.

The point about folk music, and all the Wolfe Tones' music and lyrics, is that it allows us to travel in time and experience vicariously things we could never know personally, using music subliminally, with its associations, to create emotion and image. Most of us are unlikely to get up at dawn to see the sun at 'Newgrange', and we cannot set sail in a coffin ship to an unknown future in the New World 'Lough Sheelin Eviction', wander around a harbour at night, hearing the far-off sound of sea shanties 'Child of Destiny', or be hijacked and become a South American freedom fighter 'John O'Brien' with Tijuana style brass accompaniement. Nor are we able to yomp over the Healy Pass with a flying column, scratching the Republican itch and trying to keep our spirits up by singing 'Come Out You Black and Tans'. We can be there in our imagination in a dank, dark chapel, as witnesses to Joseph Plunkett and Grace Gifford's doomed marriage 'Grace' or sit in a damp cell watching a small guttering candle while waiting to be taken out and shot 'Light a Penny Candle'. This is the power of the ballad. Today it is art. Just as opera is art. It was real once, but exists now only in our imagination. Sometimes it is not even real, like singing on the Healy Pass and not that song which wasn't written until the 1970s. The Republican itch was real however and a consequence of wearing the same clothes constantly and sharing beds never allowed to cool down! Dan Breen and Ernie O'Malley recount these anecdotes in their autobiographies.

It is this experience, superbly created and performed, that brings us to the Wolfe Tones' concerts. Nobody attending a performance of *Carmen* intends to take up bullfighting or cigar manufacture; they just come out attempting to sing opera in the bath at home. The Wolfe Tones have been around long enough to understand this, and offer the opportunity, unlike La Scala Milan and the rest, to join in at the time! This highlights another example of Brian's experience and judgment: he effectively added one such rousing chorus to 'Lough Sheelin Side' to create 'Lough Sheelin Eviction'. Interestingly, at a student performance recently, they were joining in even before the performance, as well as during it and afterwards – completely word-perfect. As Tommy pointed out in wonder in his song introduction at the time, those in the crowd weren't even born when 'Streets of New York' was at number one in the Irish charts in 1981.

According to Brian, the guide at the National Gallery, and history, 1167 is when things started to go wrong; his song 'You'll Never Beat the Irish' documents this in succinct accuracy, brilliantly, listing all the monarchs of Britain – a major achievement in itself – as well as their faults and errors. Tough on any relatives of Henry VIII to hear about him, but no doubt relief that syphilis doesn't feature. The lyrics show one aspect of his writing, with witty, cutting and accurate assessments delivered in rhyming couplets over many verses, and with another rousing chorus that is again the folk equivalent of stadium rock: clever and uplifting. It is worth googling. Its uplifting nature is key to the true supportive role of the Wolfe Tones in the North, reminding people that things work out in the end because of innate Irish qualities of character, wit being uppermost. His lyrics use the appropriate stylised vernacular of the era, they fit and they rhyme, and are funny too where intended'Helicopter Song'

*Brian remembering the
words of his fast paced
satires*

Brian's songwriting follows the example of the balladeers, recounting stories of current events and history from 1167 onwards with which he tours the world with the Wolfe Tones. We are brought up to believe nowadays that colonialism is bad because it involves domination by one nation of another and the takeover of national assets. Its defenders would say that the coloniser may bring scientific knowledge and achievements, and bring about the advance of living standards. However, it may also involve enforcement and physical force. In modern times, Roger Casement saw colonialism at first hand in the Congo administered by the Belgians, generally considered and remembered for their extreme cruelty in the early twentieth century. This would convince him to use his influence to end British colonialism in Ireland 'Lonely Banna Strand' a song brought up to date with the addition of the last verse by Derek.

Long before then, there was everyday life in Ireland to cope with, as an adjunct to the expansion of the British Empire, which required resources and was instrumental in creating nineteenth-century agricultural misery, starvation disease and emigration, changing the face of Ireland irrevocably.

This is where things start to get complicated because of the misuse of language to describe what the band do. We know that history is written by the winners: a number of terms that have several meanings have been used in a sloppy way, and convey inappropriate meaning and pejorative associations. This will become apparent as of relevance to the Broadcasting Act later.

Republicanism is a term with two meanings. Nineteen sixteen is revered as the start of the creation of the independent Irish Republic; this was delivered ultimately as a result of the efforts of the Irish Republican Brotherhood, later to become the Irish Republican Army, along with the Irish Citizen Army. Having created the Republic is celebrated as a matter of national pride. Yet relatively recent events have resulted in draconian methods of social control directed against non violent republicans. An uncle of mine once described hire purchase as 'the glad and sorry'. Glad you have got it and sorry because you have got to pay for it. There are parallels with attitudes to the Republic. The National Grave Association invited Derek to perform the songs of the volunteers at the exact hour and on the exact date April 24th that Padraic Pearse read the Proclamation at the same place outside the GPO. Watched by the crowd of 20,000 this was not televised. The official televised ceremony was on Easter Monday at the cemetery with no distinctions between combatants. Allen [1916] describes the counter-revolution of 1923 and the creation of modern Irish politics flowing from it.

The Irish Republican Army has evolved a number of times out of all recognition since then, gaining technology and losing the historical romance of 1916 – which is partly what brings audiences to the Wolfe Tones concerts. It was decommissioned and disbanded as a condition of the Good Friday agreement in 1998, possibly aided by a judgment of a European Court of Human Rights case (Purcell v. An Taoiseach), which cited it to deny election rights to the electorate with regard to Sinn Féin, the political party often described as its political wing. There is a lifetime of difference between its manifestation in 1916 and at the time of the introduction of the Broadcasting Act in 1960, and certainly Section 31 in 1976.

Similarly, there is a world of difference between people who relish the idea of the freedom of Ireland from colonial rule and those who were prepared to shoot people to achieve it.

Chapter 6

The Famine

In the nineteenth century, half of Ireland was owned by 750 people. Many had been rewarded with the land by an absentee monarch as part of a system for controlling the Irish. Many of them were absentee landlords in turn, not being connected to the land by birth or by purchase. The estates were colossal, and had tenant farmers who paid rent to a land agent. The land agents had to collect the rents, and had infrequently supervised powers, so that they could create smaller, less productive landholdings for tenants in order to increase rents. This had the effect of encouraging subsistence farming.

One infamous land agent was Captain Charles Boycott, a former army officer who was basically no good. He eventually became the agent for an estate in the North and antagonised everybody with his rigidity: the tenants had no rights and could be evicted at will 'Lough Sheelin Eviction'. A tenancy at will does not have a contract for a fixed period of time, but just the notice period of the interval between rent payments. Once they had been evicted, the neighbours could not give shelter, for fear of being evicted themselves. The evicted family had to head for a different part of the country, or emigrate 'Botany Bay' if they could afford it. Often it was a death sentence because of the lack of shelter and money, and still perilous if passage was obtained on the substandard 'coffin' ships to Australia or America. The risks of long sea journeys also led to wakes being held before departure for other emigrants, who were considered effectively dead to their families in Ireland after they had left the country.

'Emigrants Leave Ireland', engraving by Henry Doyle (1827–1892), from Mary Frances Cusack's *Illustrated History of Ireland*, 1868

The sort of thing that happened was that the tenant family would collectively clear the stones and boulders from marginal land to increase its productivity – very hard work – and then have the rent increased or the land taken back by the land agent or owner. A growing movement wanted the three Fs, fair rent, fixity of tenure, and free sale. Tenant right at valuation was not yet on the cards, later to be delivered by Parnell's efforts, involving payment to the tenant for improvement of the land.

The refusal to grant a requested rent reduction for Boycott's tenants following a bad harvest led to the serving of a process for non payment of the outstanding rent. One of the tenants resisted service, and everybody came to their aid and withdrew all social contact from Captain Boycott, including providing services. Charles Stewart Parnell, the TD for Mayo, had suggested the withdrawing of social contact as a more Christian way of dealing with people who benefited from evictions by taking over the farms, instead of shooting them. This was applied to Captain Boycott for his unpleasantness. It became a cause célèbre, being taken up by the newspapers, and eventually resulting in the army helping him to get the harvest in. The boycott, as it came to be called, extended to Dublin, and he was forced to leave the country. The term to 'boycott' entered the language, and remains in use to this day. This incident led eventually via the effective and smart vigilante defenders of tenants' rights, the Whiteboys and the Ribbon Society, to the formation of the Land League, headed by Parnell. Another successful vigilante group, the Molly Maguires, went international: they were active in Liverpool, as well as in Pennsylvania, where they protected coal miners. Some of them were hanged, but they helped many.

The early development of land-related violence may have been the inspiration for the legislation of the Insurrection Act of 1796, forbidding the taking of oaths of allegiance, carrying arms or wandering afar without good reason. Boycotting was rendered illegal by the Coercion Acts, which also outlawed conspiracies to withhold rent. Parnell himself was imprisoned in

Kilmainham Jail for this form of criminalised civil disobedience.

Another charmer was Lord Leitrim from Mohill in County Leitrim. Not an absentee landlord, he was very much in evidence strutting around and nitpicking over the maintenance of his estate, which crossed four counties and amounted to 94,534 acres, and curtailing his tenants' freedom. Nowadays it would be called hands-on micromanagement. He gave summary notice to quit on the back of rent receipts, and once handed out twenty-nine such notices in a single day. He also allegedly exercised his version of the droit de seigneur with the tenants' daughters. Although he became a notorious example of a bad landlord, closer examination of the facts reveals that he was continuing the agricultural reforms started by the previous Earl of Leitrim. Some of those evicted were reinstalled on better, but neglected farms to improve them. However, he came to embody the disrespect for the tenants of the day, including complete indifference to their welfare, although the incidents cited of him inspecting household linen and, if poorly maintained, postponing its replacement, and replacing tenants' cattle overnight without consultation, may have been misunderstood, involving paternalistic expense unknown today. He disapproved of smoking and imposed heavy fines on anyone caught doing so. His attitudes to the tenants mirrored those of his class to domestic servants not just in Ireland but also in England, as depicted in films like *Gosford Park* – working from dawn till dusk, drudgery, coerced sexual favours, summary sackings without reference, half a day a week to maintain family contact – but they at least were fed. They said he never looked back having spoken, so one can imagine the muttering that went on. There was a growing movement of dissatisfaction generally in the country, which resulted in the revision of land law; this was followed by the creation of the Irish Land Commission to give security of tenure to tenants; twenty-one-year tenancies;

compensation for summary eviction; and even assistance to buy the land for settled tenants. The importance of the development of land law cannot be overestimated because it opens the way to the monetisation of leases etc and hence the evolution of the national economy closely followed by the general improvement in living standards.

Meanwhile, in England, incompetent economic theory had imposed tariffs on imported wheat to encourage the maintenance of domestic wheat prices. However, this failed to benefit the British economy in any significant way, and led many to consider the alternative of free trade. It made bread expensive. This was a time of the expansion of the empire and industrialization, with the growth of towns and a great demand for food. Hence the export of wheat and cattle from Ireland, while tenant farmers were living at subsistence level. It is believed that Britain would have moved towards free trade in the period 1846 to 1860, even if the Irish potato famine had not occurred. When the blight attacked the food staple of the subsistence farmers, potatoes, overnight, disease, in the form of typhoid and then cholera followed hunger, and starvation and death ensued. Even so the export of food continued at gunpoint 'Hibernia'.

Both Brian and Derek each made a great study of the Famine 'Exodus' and 'Legacy' respectively, each releasing CDs, Brian sharing the opinion that the manner of dealing with the issue so ineffectively   constituted   genocide (www.wolfetonesofficialsite.co/famine/htm). The Irish potato failure, a food crisis that took place in Ireland between 1845 and 1851, led to the death of one million people as a result of starvation or disease. This tragedy coincided with the repeal of the Corn Laws by Prime Minister Robert Peel.

It is estimated that a labourer's family of four living under the conacre system of working for a tenancy of a twelve-foot-square mud cabin and half an acre of land, consumed 6 to 10 pounds (3 to 5 kilos) of potatoes each per day. This weight seems colossal and is hard to believe. It is said that the potato is the complete food, lacking only Vitamin A requiring buttermilk. The land grew the potatoes and kept a pig, which got the potato skins, but debt may have required its sale. The national dish today is cabbage and bacon with potatoes. When Peel imported Indian maize to relieve the starvation it was indigestible without sufficient bulk to fill, slow to cook and caused diarrhoea, so unsatisfactory by comparison.

Mohill has had its share of celebrities. Jonathan Swift, Dean Swift, and author of Gulliver's Travels, visited in 1732 and said, 'While the land was ill used' and 'not turned to half its advantage', it was in better shape than the people: 'the faces and habits and dwellings of the natives were so terrible' that one would 'hardly think himself in a land where law, religion or common humanity is professed'. He had a friend in the area, Turlough O'Carolan, who had a farm at Lakefield nearby, where his wife and seven children lived, while he travelled the length and breadth of Ireland as the last of the bards. When he died, in 1738, some say it ended the bardic tradition in that form. We know it continues, of course 'Carolan's Favourite', 'Carolan's Concerto'. There is a statue to him in the square, where he is known as the blind harper, and he influenced Brian to learn to play the harp, as previously mentioned, and tour the world.

Lord Leitrim believed that the British government was incompetent, with its laissez-faire policies, and campaigned hard for public works to provide income. He was instrumental in the construction of the Ballinamore-Ballyconnell canal to connect Lough Erne with the River Shannon; this project employed seven thousand men. His argument was that social outrages are committed by miserable people. He himself made many people miserable and was an aggravating member of the workhouse board.

The Society of Friends, of which Arthur Hyde, the grandfather of Douglas Hyde, later to found and become president of the Gaelic League and eventually the first President of Ireland, was a local member, was very effective in aiding the starving. The local workhouse doubled the number of its inmates between 1847 and 1850 but was mismanaged. Others helped adolescent girls respond to a request from Australia for women for unattached men, kitting them out (with clothes, and two pounds of soap each) and sending forty-five of them to Sydney in 1848 and 1850. Their descendants today go to Wolfe Tones concerts!

The morality of leaving people to die of disease and starvation is beyond description 'The Great Hunger'. The inhumanity was a feature of the time, and destitution meant the workhouse – or rather the workhouse meant destitution, because all possessions, such as there were, had to be sold to qualify for admission. This heartlessness and distorted thinking, however, were not confined to Ireland, and operated in England too, where there was the idea of the deserving and undeserving poor. A sober, respectable family, falling on hard times, might qualify for a payment from parish funds or outdoor relief instead of the workhouse. Against this, prominent respectable citizens had made money from the slave trade, which was only abolished in the British Empire in 1833. Jane Austen even alluded to this hypocrisy of respectability paid for by the immorality of slavery in one of her books, Mansfield Park. Bristol and Liverpool grew on the profits of the slave trade as important ports for the traders. Life basically was cheap, and the notion of human rights was in its infancy.

In 1796 the Prime Minister William Pitt asked Camden the Viceroy of Ireland for permission to give a peerage to "our friend Bob Smith" a member of a banking family who had assisted financially with parliamentary seats and the Prince of Wales debts'. He took the name of Carrington from a defunct Irish barony previously created for someone with the name Smith, although no relation, but remained firmly located in Nottinghamshire, rapidly gaining a British peerage. Apparently socially closer to Lord Leitrim therefore.

In 1798 Theobald Wolfe Tone founding member of the Society of United Irishmen lead the Irish Rebellion and is considered the father of Irish republicanism Disappointed at finding no support for a plan that he had submitted to William Pitt the Younger, the same, to found a military colony in Hawaii he went on with Thomas Russell and Napper Tandy to endeavour to unite Protestants like himself and Catholics to bring about Irish parliamentary reform. Their endeavours were undermined by two secret societies in Ulster that emphasised religious divide. He was to die in mysterious circumstances in prison with a throat wound given cursory medical attention.

The influence of these men, their descendants and followers would re emerge in Ulster in the twentieth century.

What did for Lord Leitrim was giving notice to quit to the local church for non payment of rent. One thousand men to prevent it were met by six thousand soldiers, but the standoff was resolved by the priest's diplomacy, transferring the debt to the land outside. The striking feature of the episode was that the climate of opinion was such that he could readily whistle up six thousand soldiers for such a contentious matter. However, the locals had had enough: it is said that they put the clocks back an hour to confound his punctuality and delay his armed escort, laming his horse so that his carriage had to stop; then, when he got out of his carriage, they shot him. When he was buried, they all turned out, and a mob, it is said locally, threw fish at his coffin as it passed by. It is not stated where they got the fish from, or why it had not been eaten before.

Meanwhile, back in England, when it did happen, repeal of the Corn Laws had a dramatic impact on the capital value of farmland in Ireland and reduced the demand for labour, as Irish lands were converted from grain production to pasture. This resulted in more evictions and emigration, sometimes with one-way tickets provided by the landowner 'Many Young Men of Twenty'. Some went from Dublin to England 'Farewell to Dublin'; others from Limerick to Canada 'Sweet Tralee'; even more went from Cobh, then known as Queenstown, to America 'Shores of America'. The cotton ships to Liverpool took emigrants cheaply to New Orleans as ballast. In Cobh, the tired travellers rested, waiting in boarding houses for the next boat. It is said that when there was overcrowding, musicians would be tipped to play music for 'sleepers awake'. The music would wake the early boarders, who would come downstairs to join the party for the craic; the tipper would then race upstairs and get in their bed!

It is calculated that 2 million people left Ireland at this time: the most common ports of destination were Boston 'A Dream of Liberty' and New Orleans. There are lists available for these major ports: Baltimore: 1820-1957; Boston: 1820-1943, New York: 1820-1957 'Goodbye Mick'; New Orleans: 1820-1952; Philadelphia: 1800-1948 'The Rambling Irishman'; San Francisco: 1893-1957. Britain received 750,000. It is estimated that the people of Irish descent in America number 40 million –

ten times the current population of Ireland [BBC may16th 2001 Americas Richard Lister bibliog]. This is the greatest concentration of people of Irish descent in the world. In America, Irish ancestry makes you Irish: the Wolfe Tones have been delighted to entertain and inform all of these people about the circumstances of their roots for 54 years at the time of writing.

Brian the showman entertaining and informing the world. Anyone who can write a song called My Heart Is in Ireland *to start a concert for the homesick and nostalgic Irish, is a showman!*

This, however, is to gloss over their influence. We can add Rhode Island to the list. A few people, like Carroll Hughes in Connecticut, have seen them practically every year. He describes the Wolfe Tones as ambassadors of Ireland and says: 'You don't go to see them, you join them.' These are not empty words. The sincerity of their patriotism has been recognized, and their message has resonated with the Irish-American community the length and breadth of the United States. An American phenomenon, the proclamation, has been invoked too. More of that later.

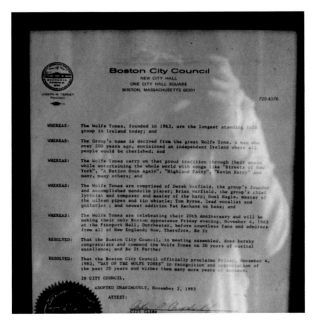

Music excellence acknowledged: For Boston City Council November 4th 1983 is "The Day of the Wolfe Tones" (Wolfe Tones archive)

The accuracy of the research behind the lyrics, carried by musical excellence, make for a powerful and memorable message, because it informs as it entertains. Keeping going for so long carries weight too. The message has been backed by charitable actions that are never referred to, such as contributions to St Patrick's Day parades, local charities, holidays for needy Irish children and medical support. No cheap publicity, but lots of appreciation.

Then, of course, there are also Canada, Australia, New Zealand, Germany, the UK, France and Bahrain, all of which are places where the Wolfe Tones have toured to packed houses over the years. In Australia, Tricia from Sydney saw them some years ago and said: 'Our friends came along thinking they were going to hear some quiet gentle music and were staggered by the enthusiasm and numbers. The cheering and singing was tribal!' In London, possibly at the National, Sylvia remembered: 'I went to see them in the 1960s – maybe early 1970s. I was a teacher in Primrose Hill then, and I went to concerts with another teacher at my school. I think we saw the Wolfe Tones in Kilburn. I remember that there were posters all over Camden Town advertising the show: they were very popular. There was a big crowd there. They were very exciting times.'

All generations loving the show London Irish Centre Camden

Very recently, also in Camden, at the London Irish Centre, Margaret saw them and said: 'I had a lovely evening. The Wolfe Tones brought revolutionary Irish history to life. The political history is an education. Everyone, including children, should hear this. Their songs are very good. It was brilliant. With Guinness too!' In Dublin in the centenary year of the Republic, Vivienne spent three days and three glorious nights with the Wolfe Tones, and said: 'The atmosphere at their concerts is unique. It's always a collective experience and the Wolfe Tones orchestrate a package of delights. It's fabulous to experience and they never miss their mark. Essentially they combine Irish musical expertise and a people's history to forge a way into the future. You get swept along with it. As they reach out to new

generations and beyond, they are a credit to their tradition.'
They are, in all but title, global ambassadors.

Michael from Glasgow experienced the Wolfe Tones at two key venues Glasgow Celtic football ground and the famous Barrowlands. He said, "At Celtic Park you can find 60,000 fans singing the Wolfe Tones. Name any other band in existence where you will find three generations of family members singing their songs together word perfect! The Wolfe Tones have always had an affiliation with Glasgow. The atmosphere inside the Barras at gigs is enough to make your hair stand on end".

Life in the towns, meanwhile, at the start of the twentieth century, was as insecure as the countryside and led eventually to the need for collective bargaining, which was resisted strongly. This is where 'James Connolly' in collaboration with Jim Larkin and the development of their union activity led to lockouts in factories in Dublin. Inappropriate violent use of the forces of law and order ultimately provoked major social change, a feature of later Irish history. The violence of the police lead to the creation of the Irish Citizen Army, and ultimately the momentous events of Easter 1916.

Chapter 7

1916: The Players

Douglas Hyde from Mohill, Leitrim, and later Frenchpark Roscommon, was directly influenced by his grandfather's work in charge of the local workhouse, undoubtedly made more difficult by one of Ireland's worst landlords, Lord Leitrim. Hyde established Conradh na Gaeilge, the Gaelic League, in collaboration with Eoin MacNeill in 1893; the aim of the organisation was to revive Irish culture and language, which was in serious decline after the drastic population reduction as a result of disease, starvation and emigration, and the imposition of English language, education and customs. Subscriptions to the organisation went from £43 in 1895 to £2,000 by 1900. Hyde resigned from Conradh na Gaeilge suddenly in 1915, possibly because its members were becoming increasingly vocal about militancy, but not before providing the intellectual, linguistic and cultural rationale for political independence, and the opportunity for the discussion of radical ideas and the impetus for change leading to the Rising. He was to go on to become the first President of Ireland.

Eoin MacNeill went on to found Óglaigh na hÉireann, the Irish Volunteers, in November 1913, as a response to the secret creation of the Ulster Volunteer Force. (The Ulster Volunteer Force, the brainchild of Sir Edward Carson and Lord Randolph Churchill, had been created out of fear of Home Rule;) it was armed and received intelligence from the British. MacNeill was to prevent the Volunteers from attending the Rising, believing it best to wait until after the war for Home Rule.

Thomas Kent from Castlelyons, Cork, joined the Gaelic League and the Irish Volunteers. One of four brothers who had drawn attention to themselves with the authorities, they disrupted a recruitment meeting called by Redmond, the leader of the Home Rule Party, by inviting Terence McSwiney to speak. Although prevented from fighting in 1916 by the orders that never arrived, he was a signatory to the Proclamation but was shot for armed resistance in Cork.

Terence McSwiney, the Mayor of Cork, was strongly opposed to conscription to the British army. He was to die on hunger strike in Brixton Prison.

Roger Casement from Dublin and Antrim was appointed British Consul to the Belgian Congo (now the Democratic Republic of Congo) in 1900. The Congo Free State was the personal territory of King Leopold II of Belgium and in 1903 Casement was asked to investigate allegations of atrocities in the rubber industry. From there he went as Consul-General to Brazil in 1906 and In 1910 he was chosen again to investigate allegations of misconduct in the rubber industry this time in the Peruvian Amazon Company (PAC) in the Putumayo region of Peru. So effective was he that he exposed the conditions to world attention and was later knighted. His observations caused him to reflect on the colonisation of Ireland by the British and the treatment of the Irish. He used his diplomatic contacts to approach the Germans for assistance for the uprising, but was captured when the weapons were jettisoned.   Executed in London the original song about him had its last verse added by Derek when his body was repatriated years later eventually Lonely Banna Strand

The seven executed signatories to the Proclamation read by Padraic Pearse outside the GPO on April 24th Easter Monday 1916 were:

James Connolly 'James Connolly' A Scottish-born labour activist, he spent some time in the British army and hated it for evermore. His socialist activities in Scotland included sharing a platform with Charlotte Despard, an acclaimed socialist speaker, feminist and humanitarian, later to be active in Ireland invited by Connolly himself.

Charlotte Despard (note the sandals and mantilla) founder of the Women's Prisoner Defence League and prominent suffragette in UK & Ireland, socialist collaborator and friend of the Connollys and the Sheehy Skeffingtons. Persuaded to speak in Ireland by James Connolly thus returned to her Irish roots. Presently in Glasnevin Cemetery finally reunited with her friends after northern reluctance to let her go (but they kept her money).

He wrote many articles for the Harp, the Irish Socialist Federation newspaper he edited, before leaving Dublin in 1903 in search of work. He sold insurance in Troy, New York, lying about his finances to get the job. He later worked as a lathe operator in the Singer Sewing Machine Company in Elizabeth,

New Jersey before becoming a national organiser for the Socialist Party of America in 1909 and 1910. He had addressed 8,000 people assembled on May Day 1908 in Union Square, near Greenwich Village. He was greatly concerned about the hypocrisy inherent in American capitalism, which favoured the wealthy while exploiting the poor, and naturally was concerned for immigrant workers. It is believed that this was pivotal in making him an outstanding leader. He returned to Dublin in 1910

James Larkin, a fellow unionist, was originally from Liverpool, and had already had considerable union success, having started the Irish Transport and General Workers Union in Belfast, and the Irish Labour Party. Through Larkin's efforts, the members obtained large pay increases in Dublin, Cork and Belfast, and the membership grew from 4,000 to 10,000 between 1911 and 1913. He was later to spend time in prison in America. Connolly had returned from America, and together they campaigned to improve working conditions in Dublin. Connolly is credited with wanting to create an Irish socialist republic and to destroy capitalism by means of the strike action of large unions. Their initial target was to improve conditions in a Dublin factory; the dispute resulted in a lockout and a large riot, in which 450 were injured and one person died. This day was known as Bloody Sunday (the first time the term was used). The violence from the police, on behalf of a worried owner class, resulted in the creation of the Irish Citizen Army, who were available for the rebellion, along with the women's organisation Cumman na mBan 'Women of Ireland', 'Margaret Skinnider'. In all, 1,200 men and women, from the Irish Volunteers, the Irish Citizen Army and Cumman na mBan, took part in the Rising.

Padraic Pearse 'Padraic Pearse' was born in Dublin and joined the Gaelic League in 1895, becoming a member of the Executive Committee in 1898. He studied law at University College Dublin, graduating in 1901 with a degree in Arts and Law and going on to become a barrister. He cared passionately about the Irish language and culture. He edited the Gaelic League newspaper An Claidheamh Soluis ('Sword of Light') and went on to lecture in Irish at UCD. With Thomas MacDonagh, he set up a bilingual school for boys, St Enda's in Ranelagh, Dublin; the school moved to Rathfarnham in 1910.

Joseph Mary Plunkett, born into a wealthy republican Dublin family, was considered the primary military tactician of the Rising. He contemplated becoming a professional skater, apparently being particularly proficient. Along with Pearse and Éamonn Ceannt, he conducted a feasibility study into holding an insurrection in Ireland as early as October 1914. He travelled to Germany in 1915 to link up with Roger Casement to raise an Irish Brigade from among Irish prisoners of war in Germany. An experienced traveler, he had the excuse that he needed to travel abroad for his health, so was the best placed of them all to travel to Germany in wartime. Under the pretence of travelling to Jersey, Plunkett went to Germany via Spain in March 1915 via a long, scenic route. Knowing the seriousness of the mission, he even destroyed every known photograph of himself beforehand. He married Grace Gifford in Kilmainham Jail chapel, on the eve of his execution after the Rising 'Grace'.

Seán Mac Diarmada was born John McDermott in January 1883, at Kiltyclogher, barely 60 kilometres from Mohill in County Leitrim. It is almost certain therefore that he had heard of Lord Leitrim, if his family had not been tenants of the estate. He was the eighth child of carpenter Donald McDermott and his wife Mary. An obituary of his father published in 1913 in the radical newspaper Irish Freedom claimed that Donald was not only a veteran of the Land League, but that he 'was one of Ireland's true sons and one of those men who, guided by high principles and an ardent love of his country, took his place in the ranks of the IRB'. He himself had joined the Irish Republican Brotherhood in 1906 and was co-opted onto the Supreme Council in 1908, so it was not surprising that he became manager of Irish Freedom in 1910. The newspaper sought to advance and promote the political aspirations of the IRB, and did not mince its words: 'The Irish attitude to England is war yesterday, war today, war tomorrow. Peace after the final battle.' Mac Diarmada became particularly close to Thomas Clarke.

Thomas Clarke, a veteran Fenian, had been imprisoned for his involvement in the dynamite campaign of the 1880s. He was born on the Isle of Wight, the son of Irish parents. His father was in the British army; the family ultimately lived in Dungannon, County Tyrone. In 1882, he emigrated to America. During his time there he joined the republican organisation Clan na Gael; as a proponent of violent revolution, he would serve fifteen years in British jails for his role in a bombing campaign in London. Where the others could appear as poets and dreamers, Clarke was an unequivocally 'hard man'. Allegedly responsible for the Phoenix Park murders, it was his actions that led to the setting up of the London Metropolitan Police 'Special Irish Branch' to monitor republican activities.

Eamon Ceannt was a founder member of the Irish Volunteers and worked for Dublin City Council. He was elected to the provisional committee, becoming involved in fundraising for arms.

Thomas MacDonagh was born in Tipperary and trained as a priest but, like both his parents, became a teacher, and was on the staff at St Enda's, the school he helped to found with Padraic Pearse. In 1909 he was a founding member of the Association of Secondary Teachers of Ireland (ASTI), and was also involved in setting up, in 1911, the Irish Women's Franchise League, which promoted Irish nationalism and the cultural revival. A gifted poet, writer and dramatist, his play When the Dawn Is Come was produced at the Abbey Theatre. He joined the Irish Volunteers in November 1913, becoming a member of the provisional committee and taking part in the Howth gun-running. He believed Irish freedom would be achieved by what he called 'zealous martyrs'; if necessary, by war. Although a member of the IRB from April 1915, MacDonagh was not co-opted to the Military Council until early April 1916, and so played little part in planning the Rising 'The Road to the Rising'. He is believed, however, to have contributed to the content of the Proclamation. One of his two most senior officers was **Major John MacBride** (husband of **Maud Gonne)**. MacDonagh was executed by firing squad at Kilmainham Jail on 3 May 1916.

The seven signatories of the 1916 Proclamation constituted the entire military council of the Irish Republican Brotherhood at that time. The IRB, effectively a mixture of Fenians, intellectuals and Marxist union membership, was dedicated to the use of force against England at any favourable opportunity, echoing the Fenian position of independence and democracy achieved by necessary violence, believing that Ireland would never be relinquished peacefully. 'The One Road', 'Ireland Unfree Shall Never Be at Peace'

Sam Maguire from Dunmanway in Cork was a member of the IRB. In 1909 he inducted **Michael Collins** 'Michael Collins' into the IRB. Collins had been pursuing a career in financial services, firstly in London, then in New York, and subsequently with a firm of stockbrokers in Dublin. Maguire is credited with the development of Gaelic football:

On 1 November 1884 the Gaelic Athletic Association was founded at Miss Hayes' Commercial Hotel, Thurles, Co. Tipperary, by Michael Cusack [Clareman, teacher, sportsman and nationalist] and Maurice Davin [a Tipperary man who at the time was Ireland's most famous athlete]. Other founding members present were John Wyse-Power, John McKay, J. K. Bracken, Joseph O'Ryan and Thomas St George McCarthy. Many of the seven men who attended the meeting were Fenians. Not present at the Thurles meeting was Patrick W. Nally, a keen athlete and leading IRB organiser who also played a prominent role in bringing about the birth of the GAA: he was the one who suggested the organisation to Cusack.' [Wikipedia see Pat Nally]

Sam Maguire was prominent and highly successful in the London branch of the GAA but left in a hurry after a tip off. For many years he was one of Collins's right-hand men. As Collins's chief intelligence officer in London, Maguire was to become the centre of Scotland Yard's investigation into the assassination in June 1922 of Sir Henry Wilson, the man responsible for setting up the Cairo Gang (see Chapter 8). While working in the Irish Civil Service, he had serious political differences with his line manager and was sacked without a pension; he died young of TB, in straitened circumstances. The national Gaelic football trophy is named after him. He is, in short, in the pantheon of heroes.

The early effect of the new Irish consciousness manifested itself with an interest in ancient celtic sport as well as culture.

The Gaelic Athletics Association started to provide recreation and revive the sport of hurling. The success of this entertainment is credited with bringing about new Irish pride in popular thought known as 'the Celtic Dawn', as well as providing opportunities for improving physical fitness – something which would prove to be very useful later to the Volunteers who used the fitness programmes for the "sport".

These people meant business! The trigger for action was the war with Germany and the creation of the UVF, which was already buying weapons abroad. The serious threat was the possibility of conscription. Although neutral, the expression 'England's difficulty is Ireland's opportunity' was very much to the fore. Casement and Plunkett in Germany explored the possibility of recruiting men and obtaining weapons for the Rising, with the hope of creating an Irish Brigade of Irishmen incarcerated in Germany. In the event, they only recruited fifty-five. The Germans sent a shipment of more than 20,000 captured Russian rifles, ten machine-guns and 4 million rounds of ammunition to aid the Irish, but they were dumped to avoid capture, before they could be handed over at Fenit Harbour in County Kerry.

The unknown quantity was German intentions. Casement believed they were genuine in their desire to assist, or at least that his contact was. After the failure of the Rising a second shipment was planned in 1917, but it did not materialise. What they did not know was that in production, presumably in secret, was the Paris gun, which was not deployed until 1918. It had a range of 81 miles. It was used to demoralise Paris, not being considered accurate for anything smaller than cities. If the Rising had been successful, positioning the length of the east coast of Ireland could have demoralised the west coast of England: the gun would have been in range of Cardiff and Liverpool, weakening the British war effort. In the event, the ship, originally an English merchant vessel, captured by the

Germans in 1914, masqueraded as the Aud disguised as a Norwegian freighter. It was eventually scuppered in Cork harbour while under naval escort. The volunteer crew and captain survived and were interned.

Meanwhile, **Eamon de Valera**, born in Manhattan and raised in Limerick, got a pass degree in mathematics at UCD and became a maths professor at Belvedere College. He was inducted into the IRB in 1909 by Thomas McDonagh. In 1916 he commanded the garrison at Boland's Mills. Sentenced to death for his role in the Rising, this was later commuted to life imprisonment, but he was released in June 1917. It is said that his American status saved him from the firing squad, but also the tide of public opinion had turned. Between June 1919 and December 1920 he was to raise $6 million in America for a future Irish government.

The specific events of the uprising are well documented. Brave people did their best and many died 'The Foggy Dew'. In so doing, they delivered the Proclamation, outlining their goals 'The Road to the Rising'. This had been read from the headquarters at the General Post Office on Easter Monday April 24th 1916 by Padraic Pearse.

One goal concerning the equality of women was to be immediately set aside by Eamon de Valera and others. Someone possibly eliminated **Elizabeth O'Farrell**, the nurse, from the historic photograph of the surrender, and generally they under emphasised the role of the women.

Notable amongst the women who played an active part in the Rising was **Countess Markievicz, née Gore Booth**, a communist who was up there with the 'menfolk'. Not to mock her intellectual rigour, she is said to have fashioned a uniform for herself by modifying one of the rebel's shirts. She wrote a pamphlet reproduced in the National Library of Ireland's Revolution Paper reprints (No. 59) of the media of the era. Her parents investigated and declared her husband's Polish title spurious. Reports make her sound quite irritating, and trivialise her, quoting her advice that women thinking of getting involved should wear shorter skirts strong boots and carry a pistol, actually probably quite good advice. She is said to have assisted Charlotte Despard's initiative feeding the families of strikers and prisoners, continuing her prominent family's sense of responsibility that had ensured the tenants were fed throughout the difficult years unlike those of other estates. She was saved from the firing squad because she was a woman. Sexism has its advantages.

Charlotte Despard, sister of – and politically, diametrically opposed to – Field Marshall French, the future Lord Lieutenant of Ireland, was a leading British suffragette who founded welfare centres in Nine Elms, London with her own money. The Sheehy Skeffingtons were her friends, as supporters of the women's suffrage movement before 1916, and Hanna remained so after Francis was shot. Despard spent a great deal of time in Ireland and in 1908 had joined **with Hanna Sheehy Skeffington and Margaret Cousins** to form the Irish Women's Franchise League (WFL). In 1909 Despard met Gandhi and was influenced by his theory of 'passive resistance'. As the leading figure of the WFL, she urged members not to pay taxes and to boycott the 1911 Census in Britain.

Charlotte Despard may not have made the sandwiches herself during the Lockout period, being already very old, but paid expenses. 'They also serve who only sit and wait.' She helped establish the Irish Workers' College in the city. She was later to start the Women's Prisoners' Defence League with **Maud**

Gonne to assist the families left without support after the men were arrested. After the end of the First World War she became a supporter of Sinn Féin and participated in the Labour Party Commission of Inquiry into the atrocities committed by the police and army. The pair were known as 'Maud Gonne Mad' and 'Charlotte Desperate', both preceded by the title 'Madame', which set them apart.

Also active post-Rising was **Mary McSwiney,** the widow of Terence. She was eventually elected to the Dáil.

The proclamation read by Pearse was not the first proclamation in support of a republic: the first had been written by **Robert Emmet,** a friend of **Wolfe Tone.** Emmet had revived the United Irish Society and had organised an uprising that also failed due to firearms that had been promised not being supplied. His uprising also went ahead in Dublin, on the evening of 23 July 1803. About 10,000 copies of his proclamation were printed, in the name of the 'Provisional Government'. He was eventually arrested and hanged, then beheaded. His speech from the dock after his barrister was bought off and his assistant took over is famous: 'When my country takes her place among the nations of the earth, then and not till then, let my epitaph be written.' He could have escaped from Ireland but came back to see his one true love his girlfriend Sarah Curran, bringing with him his loyal housekeeper Anne Devlin 'Anne Devlin of the Hills'. On the subject of proclamations the Wolfe Tones were the recipients of congratulatory proclamations themselves or illuminated addresses, the existence of which were to be persuasive of the grassroots in America and therefore the politicians too.

Kansas City Proclamation February 23rd 1990 is Wolfe Tones Day
Wolfe Tones Archive

The significant factor was the violent behaviour of the British army, which stirred up an otherwise passive population to take the side of the Republic. They might have had the excuse of post traumatic stress disorder [PTSD] if it had been known to medical science at the time. Civilians were tried without defence representation and the ringleaders executed, in the manner of deserters from the army in a state of war. This included James Joyce's friend **Francis Sheehy Skeffington,** a known pacifist who was apparently only there by accident, having been brought in by a patrol while trying to stop the looting. The officer concerned was allegedly suffering some kind of religious fugue, making the soldiers kneel in prayer so the story goes, a possible candidate for a PTSD diagnosis.

Hanna Sheehy Skeffington recounted her experiences to Haydon Talbot which were shocking about the targetting of Francis and 50 others by the officer responsible for his execution who was later court martialled and confined to a psychiatric hospital but released later for not being insane. She lectured in America after escaping in various disguises via Scotland and was constantly followed, an attempt even being made to lure her to the dominion of Canada to deport her.

What really disgusted the general population was that James Connolly, who was dying of gangrene from a gunshot wound to his leg, was brought by ambulance to Kilmainham Jail, where the Rising leaders were held, and tied to a chair to hold him upright so that he could be shot ('The Dying Rebel').

Some thought that General Sir John Maxwell should have been next. His actions were set against the new Defence of the Realm Act of August 1914: 'No person shall by word of mouth or in writing spread reports likely to cause disaffection or alarm among any of His Majesty's forces or among the civilian population.' The trivial peacetime activities no longer permitted included flying kites, starting bonfires, buying binoculars, feeding wild animals bread, discussing naval and military matters, and buying alcohol on public transport. Alcoholic beverages were watered down and opening times were restricted to noon to 3 pm and 6.30 to 9.30 pm... 'and may, by such regulations, authorise the trial by courts martial and punishment of persons contravening any of the provisions of such regulations', specifically '1(a) to prevent persons communicating with the enemy or obtaining information for that purpose or any purpose calculated to jeopardise the success of the operations of any of His Majesty's forces or the forces of his allies or to assist the enemy'.

The Wikipedia entry on Maxwell is worth quoting: 'he set about dealing with the rebellion under his understanding of martial law. During the week 2 to 9 May, Maxwell was in sole charge of trials and sentences by "field general court martial", which was trial without defence or jury and in camera. He had 3,400 people arrested, 183 civilians tried, 90 of whom were sentenced to death. Fifteen were shot between 3 and 12 May."

Prime Minister Asquith and his government became concerned at the speed and secrecy of events before intervening to stop more executions. In particular, there was concern that DORA regulations for general courts martial were not applied. These regulations called for a full court of thirteen members, a professional judge, a legal advocate and the case being heard in public, which could have prevented some executions. Maxwell admitted in a report to Asquith in June that the impression that the leaders were killed in cold blood without trial had resulted in a 'revulsion of feeling' that had set in, in favour of the rebels, and was the result of the confusion between applying DORA as opposed to martial law (for which Maxwell had actually pressed from the beginning). Although Asquith promised to publish the court-martial proceedings, they were not published until the 1990s. The awfulness of the treatment meant that they did not die in vain consequently.

19 children were shot in the head as reported in the pathologists's report in the RTE docudrama of the "trial" of Padraic Pearse. A very high percentage suggesting the deliberate targeting of children.

Even a tender moment among the uniforms, the wedding of **Grace Gifford,** from a well-connected Dublin family and **Joseph Mary Plunkett,** a signatory of the Proclamation 'Grace', ended badly. Grace Gifford had apparently told the priest she was pregnant, in order to ask him to intercede so that the marriage could take place. As was customary, the condemned were invited to make a will while awaiting execution 'Light a Penny Candle', which he did. Unfortunately this was before the wedding, and he was not advised that marriage negates previous wills. After his death his wealthy family challenged the will, and in the end Grace, who did not have a child, settled for a very modest lump sum and lived alone in a room for the rest of her life. She had been studying art prior to the engagement, and during the civil war was at one time detained in Kilmainham Jail herself, under her married name. Known to have participated in the graffiti custom in Kilmainham Jail, given her status and expertise, as well as her political sophistication, she may well have directed the creation of the famous legend above the door in the corridor, where it is written: 'Beware of the risen people harried and held Ye that have bullied and bribed.'

Women's Wing Kilmainham Jail mural "Beware of the Risen People"

This is taken from Padraic Pearse's poem 'The Rebel' later set to music by Brian.

The Rebel (Pearse)

I am come of the seed of the people, the people that sorrow;
Who have no treasure but hope,
No riches laid up but a memory of an ancient glory
My mother bore me in bondage, in bondage my mother was born,
I am of the blood of serfs;
The children with whom I have played, the men and women with whom I have eaten
Have had masters over them, have been under the lash of masters,
and though gentle, have served churls.
The hands that have touched mine,
the dear hands whose touch Is familiar to me
Have worn shameful manacles, have been bitten at the wrist by manacles,
have grown hard with the manacles and the taskwork
of strangers.
I am flesh of the flesh of these lowly, I am bone of their bone I
that have never submitted;
I that have a soul greater than the souls of my people's masters,
I that have vision and prophecy, and the gift of fiery speech,
I that have spoken with God on the top of his holy hill.
And because I am of the people, I understand the people,
I am sorrowful with their sorrow, I am hungry with their desire;
My heart is heavy with the grief of mothers,
My eyes have been wet with the tears of children,
I have yearned with old wistful men,
And laughed and cursed with young men;
Their shame is my shame, and I have reddened for it
Reddened for that they have served, they who should be free
Reddened for that they have gone in want, while others have been full,

Reddened for that they have walked in fear of lawyers and their
jailors.
With their Writs of Summons and their handcuffs,
Men mean and cruel.
I could have borne stripes on my body
Rather than this shame of my people.
And now I speak, being full of vision:
I speak to my people, and I speak in my people's name to
The masters of my people:
I say to my people that they are holy,
That they are august despite their chains.
That they are greater than those that hold them
And stronger and purer,
That they have but need of courage, and to call on the name of
their God,
God the unforgetting, the dear God who loves the people
For whom he died naked, suffering shame.
And I say to my people's masters: Beware
Beware of the thing that is coming, beware of the risen people
Who shall take what ye would not give.
Did ye think to conquer the people, or that law is stronger than
life,
And than men's desire to be free?
We will try it out with you ye that have harried and held,
Ye that have bullied and bribed.
Tyrants… hypocrites… liars!

Retrieved from
"https://en.wikisource.org/w/index.php?title=The_Rebel_(Pears
e)&oldid=6206399"

The Wolfe Tones have a reputation, even among people who
don't know them, for their songs about 1916 which gives them
the romantic allure of doomed idealism. Opponents of

Republicanism are only too ready to try to associate them with the bombs of the 1970s. The truth of their appeal lies in the tremendous breadth and range of their folk songs and ballads and the variety of styles. Being patriots it has been a long held wish to keep going long enough to commemorate the centenary of the birth of the Republic. Strangely they were enabled to do this, spectacularly, by the hiatus in their recording which gave Brian the space to write songs especially for the occasion, with a new CD *The Dublin Rebellion 1916* which involved a third collaboration with Kiev Connolly, and the Celtic Symphony Orchestra recorded with Celtic Collections. When the Wolfe Tones celebrated the centenary in Dublin achieving a long held ambition the enthusiasm of the audience, and its truly international nature, was striking.

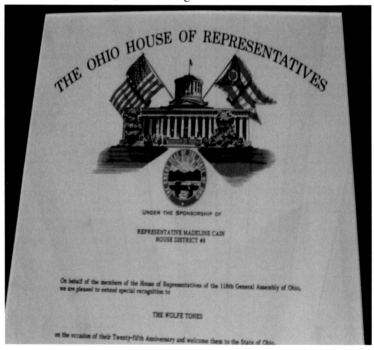

Beautiful headed document from Ohio House of Representatives praising the Wolfe Tones and congratulating them on their 25th anniversary (Wolfe Tones Archive)

Dublin Centenary concert 2016 in Irish Volunteer uniform

Brian in an Irish Volunteer cap

Martial law was declared, and in the teeth of official advice, and ignoring official requests, General Sir John Maxwell relentlessly had all the ringleaders shot, and then went round the country looking for, and arresting, sympathisers causing significant hardship.

More people were arrested in this period than took part in The Rising. This galvanised the population into rebellion against the institutions of British rule. In the elections held at the end of 1918 there was a landslide victory for Sinn Féin, which had previously been on the verge of collapse. Many Sinn Féin representatives were elected but, by refusing to go to Westminster, they effectively created an Irish parliament, which was declared to be Dáil Éireann. The IRA enforced support for this alternative government.

Violence escalated, with the IRA freeing republican prisoners around the country, but when Sinn Féin and Dáil Éireann were banned, open warfare followed, with an all-out attack on police stations, army patrols and British institutions of government 'The Boys of the Old Brigade'. To support the police, the British sent recruits, issued with combination uniforms, which gave then the infamous nickname the 'Black and Tans' 'Come Out You Black and Tans'. The War of Independence was fought between 1919 and 1921.

Seán Keating (1889 – 1977)
Men of the South
Oil on canvas 127.00 x 203.40 cm
Collection: Crawford Art Gallery, Cork

The first version of this painting is in private ownership and included the first
leader of the North Cork IRA Sean Moylan but he declined later. In this
version Michael Sullivan, John Jones, Roger Kiely, Dan Brown, Jim
O'Riordan, Denis O'Mullane, Jim Cashman may be presumed mostly.

Chapter 8

The Rift

One of the reasons the civil war was so damaging to Ireland was that, in a manoeuvre that could have created the expression 'fiendishly clever', but continuing a tradition of long duration, Irish men continued to be recruited into the army following the withdrawal of the infamous Black and Tans, noted for their deliberately unreasonable and ultimately ineffectual cruelty, from Ireland. The Irishmen were transferred to the Free State army, believing they were fighting for Ireland.

The issue was whether Ireland wanted to be part of the British Empire or not. Eamon de Valera, formerly the head of the revived Sinn Féin, now putative President of Dáil Éireann, the de facto Irish government, said not. The Anglo-Irish Treaty made allegiance to the monarchy and membership of the Empire compulsory, as a dominion, like Canada and Australia.

Michael Collins had been sent to Britain, despite his protestations to de Valera about his lack of experience, to negotiate. De Valera may have identified something later discovered by psychologists: in hostage situations, the decision maker must not negotiate directly, and conversely, the negotiator must not make decisions but must defer back. This went wrong, famously, and the six counties of the North were allowed to be set apart, with the agreement of Collins, who believed that this was the best possible result in a bad situation, as a starting point for the future – a decision that was to result in his assassination. The civil war, of pro- and anti-Treaty forces, ensued. Men who had previously been united against the police force found themselves on opposite sides – with the significant difference that they both had knowledge of guerrilla tactics, previously known only to the Irish Republican Army. They knew who opposed the Treaty, and they knew the Volunteers' hiding places. The fear was that the British army would be sent to 'lend a hand', and then stay, if there was an unreasonable delay in taking control. Legislation, in the form of the Public Safety Bill, made possible a campaign of murderous anarchy and summary execution. The Free State army was being supplied by Britain and had superior numbers and equipment.

This was a period of unbridled and unprincipled brutality by the Free State army although there were atrocities on both sides. In an infamous incident, a group of 9 IRA volunteers were rounded up and tied together in Ballyseedy, and then a grenade was thrown into their midst, resulting in the deaths of all of them except one, who did not speak of it for many years afterwards.

The tragedy of this period of Irish history was that it split families, and there were savage cases of brother against brother. This was something mourned by the artist Sean Keating, who depicted himself, in the painting *An Allegory*, slumped against a tree, surrounded by representatives of Irish society, in front of a burned-out Ascendancy house previously occupied by Protestants. Keating had previously painted significant soldiers of the rebellion in his painting *Men of the South*. He sneaked them into his workplace until the caretaker complained about the guns, whereupon he had to move everyone to his studio. All under the noses of the occupying forces.

In *An Allegory*, two opposing men are temporarily united, to bury someone in the name of Ireland. Look carefully at the physical features, especially the noses, and it can be surmised that they are brothers.

An Allegory, 1924 - Presented, Friends of the National Collections of Ireland, 1952, National Gallery of Ireland Collection, Photo © National Gallery of Ireland© Estate of Sean Keating, IVARO Dublin 2017

When brothers fall out, it is said to be always more savage than strangers, because they have guerrilla knowledge of each other and know how to hurt. This could be said to be true of the fallout between Derek and Brian and could be of much longer duration than a mere contract dispute. However savage things get, it is not an Irish characteristic to speak publicly against family members, but the consequences for the Wolfe Tones had to be explained to the public.

Working relationships with relatives frequently follow the pattern of family interaction. Brian was an exceptional young boy to be so highly motivated to learn about Irish culture and music that he learnt to play the harp, tin whistle, banjo, *bhodrán* and pipes. As the elder brother, Derek would have felt entitled to tell Brian what to do. Growing up in a fiercely patriotic family that played music all the time, there would have been great pressure and desire to join in. The easy, loyal option would be to learn from their father, in his case the mandolin – a delightful but unusual instrument. As a stringed instrument, the principles would be the same as other stringed instruments but the sound was different – and different from the other instruments in which Brian had become proficient. Derek had actually been given the mandolin by his grandmother when he was eight.

The concert-playing of Brian and Noel would be an incentive too to earn money, hence the formation of Derek's the Circle Group – although it is not known what kind of music they played. Hard to see it not being traditional Irish, in the circumstances! The Circle Group was Derek Warfield, Dan Maher, Terry Corcoran, and Philip Woodcut, later to play with the Wolfe Tones for a time in the early days.

Later too Brian's song writing and success for the Wolfe Tones with The Helicopter Song an acclaimed satire and the fastest ever selling single in Ireland, might have encouraged Derek to write more as well. The discovery of the Irish-American diaspora was a great incentive to all Irish musicians because of the huge, ready-made audience that existed: this audience longed to hear songs reflecting their loyalty to their ancestors, and the privations they had endured, that they themselves might prosper and be happy. So many songs in Ireland already written reflected the Irish end of the experience, but the mercenary tradition of the Irish, such as the Wild Geese in France of the defeated Jacobite army, would provide a large area of potential material in the Americas instead for songwriting that was unique to Derek – and which he pursued enthusiastically. As the Wolfe Tones' – and Brian's – catalogue of successful songs increased, so Derek wrote and recorded establishing his own reputation. It made commercial sense to seek areas that were untouched already by Brian and the Wolfe Tones, to avoid unnecessary competition while remaining true to the historical achievements of the Irish.

Concerning the sound of the band, originally authenticity was everything. Going electric would be anathema. It would be natural for Derek, as the elder brother, to want to take lead vocal, having a sweet voice – even though, at the other end of the stage, they had the immense talent of Tommy hiding behind facial hair and glasses, Derek also had the confidence to introduce the background to the songs too. He developed a traditional vocal style that in England was sometimes accompanied by a finger in the ear a capella and a strong local accent. For some reason in England it seemed it was always the singer's version of an 18th century rural Dorset accent although they themselves were 20th century urban. Traditional ethnic in other words to its devotees and beloved in America but possibly underestimating the charm of an authentic contemporary Dublin accent being surrounded by them on a daily basis. Quite different from Tommy's lyrical subtlety and diction. Musically restricted in the pursuit of authenticity compared to what Brian's musical arrangements would later become but unquestionably high quality musical renditions of traditional folk. So when he was to say later that they had musical differences, it was true, and started with the fundamentals of the sound but in fact they had all evolved their musical style considerably with the immense experience gained over time.

At a time when finally the inequalities in the north had been acknowledged and were starting to be addressed administratively it was natural to wonder where next for the band. Unfunny much repeated suggestions that they decommission their instruments accordingly highlighted the perception perhaps of a rut. Long held musical ambitions could be recognised and diametric differences started to become more pressing. An enduring difficulty following directly from Section 31 of the Broadcasting Act was the interference from Ireland in their professional lives in America. One example was the complaint from a politician in the north about a historic song written over a century previously being played on an aircraft. The fact it had been voted the best single ever in a world wide BBC poll counted for nothing. They had found it difficult to organise distribution consequently and were restricted by having to take the merchandise with them.

The success of the band continued apace however and the demand for concerts relentless. Tommy referred to them being on tour for eleven months of the year. At this time their ages would have had most people winding down their activities pre retirement. Derek's enthusiasm continued unabated for songs about the Irish in America and particularly in the War of

Independence and the Civil War whereas the others were thinking about peacetime in Ireland.

Brian, on the other hand, had been wanting to develop his ideas of arrangements influenced more in the direction of film music like Ennio Morricone's whilst retaining its folk character. The fact that Derek had been acknowledged in unchallenged record sleeve notes as the leader since the beginning created undercurrents of dissension. Derek's attempts to persuade the others to record new material were strongly resisted therefore. The richness and complexity of the Wolfe Tones style of work would have involved enormous planning and rehearsal so not being that fussed about the subject matter would have discouraged them. In actual fact many of the Irish songs in America were Irish melodies with the words changed to suit the circumstances. So he carried on without them dealing with Shanachie an acknowledged American recording company with a track record for promoting Irish bands.

He had already recorded his own music in his spare time. They offered a generous contract for US distribution of the Wolfe Tones back catalogue and he believed it did not affect the band's future recordings. He wasn't to know that Brian had been approached by an Irish company similarly interested who would record Brian's own music. Derek believes that both in fact could have been accommodated technically with the master discs being just loaned to Shanachie. A meeting took place between Shanachie, Derek and an american promotions company. Despite being pleased initially to be releasing in America it came to nothing however.

The Irish-American songs took more of his time, and he recorded his own CDs of these songs while continuing to tour with the Wolfe Tones. Personal influence and lack of enthusiasm might explain why the Wolfe Tones did not record for a significant period of time, although Derek was to say that he tried, unsuccessfully, to persuade them to do so. Perhaps the nature of the songs concerned was the reason. Pursuing his own recording career would take Derek to the same recording company in America, Shanachie, as all the Irish artists who were aiming for the American market. Having spent years introducing all the songs, with their explanations, with great success, and seemingly taking many of the lead vocals, it would have been tempting to believe that he spoke for the band, and he signed a contract. The nature of the contract, however, remains a mystery that it could deliberately restrict distribution of the Wolfe Tones material, and for years to the recording company in America. The answer could simply be a refusal to be corralled.

At this point, the subject of filthy lucre raises its head. When things go wrong for bands, it is usually at the hands of the accountants, lawyers and managers, who cream off production expenses and service charges. There is also the payment of recording and performance royalties to songwriters. Over the years, the Wolfe Tones have gradually regained control of their back catalogue and production. The question is whether Derek had independent legal advice, because the terms were deemed to be highly unsatisfactory, and completely restrictive, to the rest of the band. Did he believe that they had stopped recording? Did he want to change the pattern of control over production, publishing and royalties on his own songs, and hence income? We will never know for certain.

The dilemma was how do you tell your brother you don't want to carry on working with him after 37 highly successful years together? A personal conversation or an impersonal communication? Would he accept it and what were the implications? In the end they settled for a personal written letter which missed the benefits of each strategy. The french have an expression "If you want to kill a dog you say it has rabies" They criticised his time spent with his own recordings and set conditions he would be bound to refuse. Five minutes with an employment lawyer would have pointed out that they appear to be each self employed as is the custom in the music industry so when not involved with priority Wolfe Tones activities were each available for weddings, bar mitzfahs or high profile concerts as they chose.

What they had the sense to realise, however, was that without getting expensively legal the letter communicated the simple information that they didn't want to work with him any more. End of. The association had endured longer than most marriages and vastly longer than most in the industry. It represented a major achievement. Unfortunately it left a nasty taste in the mouth.

A standoff followed which lasted for several years and they argued over who had the right to the name. This is where working with relatives is dangerous, because there is a danger of glossing over the kind of details that create difficulties later and should have been subject to contractual clarity.

When an object is thrown in a pond, its dimensions can be calculated to a certain extent by measuring the depth and width of the ripples. The consequences of the fallout were far-reaching and painful. Firstly, each excised the other from any documentary evidence on their websites, so it was as though they had never existed. Then there was the 'battle of the copyrights', where every arrangement was copyrighted, if the authorship could not be; this applied to music and words too. The situation reached such a pitch that Tommy and Noel were overlooked, despite their key roles. CDs were recorded as private projects and both produced work on the Famine: Brian's commissioned work for Glasgow Celtic Football Club was followed by Derek's work on Glasgow Celtic Football Club songs, with no mention of Brian.

More seriously, the dispute continued as to who had the right to continue using the name 'the Wolfe Tones'. Derek's work frequently referred to 'my band', even though Brian and Noel described the start of the group at an earlier point. It was hard not to be territorial after thirty-seven years spent as the front-man, perhaps. This episode was the subject of interviews too:

> 7 Aug 2009 " 'He's going around the place using our name and that's just misleading the people who go to see his gigs,' Brian Warfield told the Irish Independent last night. 'He doesn't let people know that when they buy his tickets they're only going to see one original member of The Wolfe Tones playing with new musicians.' He said that Derek was the one who decided to set out on his own nine years ago, after deciding he wanted to do things his way.

As far as Brian is concerned, only he and the other original members of the band musician Noel Nagle and ballad singer Tommy Byrne have the right to use the Wolfe Tone name."
Derek, however, had another tale to tell.
" 'Just because my brother pulled a fast one on me and legally registered the name of the band doesn't mean he owns it,' he said yesterday.

'The name Wolfe Tone is bigger than all of us. It's about a sense of Irish tradition and heritage which I am passionate about.' Derek (66) said he became embroiled in a bitter row live on air on RTE's 'Liveline' show unawares. 'This all started because I got on to talk about Frankie Gavin, a former member of De Dannan, and his right to use the band's name for his new group,' he said."

During this period they had each discovered the name "The Wolfe Tones" was their reputation being greater than the sum of its parts. So in the end they share it.

Derek maintained that he had always wanted to record whereas the others did not, but after this they didn't record for several years. Injunctions are only temporary measures until a court hearing, so one must assume that as Derek had refused to assist in getting the contract set aside, the others would not be forced into working for a scenario they had not endorsed, and so waited for the contractual period of time to expire.

Brian the cheerleader, assisted by his daughter Siobhan and Kiev Connolly, enjoying the moment

As it happened, this period of negativity produced great benefit to both parties. Derek recorded more CDs. He also persuaded Dolphin Records to release much of the back-catalogue of the Wolfe Tones under the name 'Derek Warfield and The Wolfe

Tones' *Fifty Great Irish Rebel Songs* being no longer a member of the band itself.

Brian had worked on his song repertoire during the fallow period, and created the group's arrangements, unfettered by Derek's influence. The Wolfe Tones eventually released *Child of Destiny* with thoughtful and subtle arrangements; the title song was shared with and amended by his daughter Siobhan, a recording artist in her own right.

More recently, Derek found some young talented musicians, and he now tours with them under the name 'The Young Wolfe Tones'. In May 2011, Derek and The Young Wolfe Tones completed an extensive musical tour of Australia, appearing at the world-famous Australian National Folk Festival, to launch a commissioned new and multi toned CD, which was released the following month in Ireland, America and the UK. As he describes it: *Far Away in Australia* is a musical story of Ireland and Australia, and the contributions and historical involvement of the Irish race in Australia. The ballads in Irish traditional music are carefully chosen to reflect the many aspects of the literary, cultural, social and political that connect the two nations.'

His output is prolific and successful, and also features the songs about starving Irish mercenaries who did not get paid, and many others from whom the Irish-American community is descended. They played at the White House before the end of Barack Obama's presidency.

Musically, the split offers both great diversity of style to Wolfe Tones fans and consistent quality. Early songs were rerecorded as necessary, with new arrangements, a case in point being 'The Foggy Dew', written by Canon O'Neil, which gained a powerful atmospheric treatment with Noel's introduction. They have recorded this song at least three times, and it demonstrates the evolution of their musical style. It was the title track of their first vinyl LP, and then featured Derek's distinctive folk vocal style, and subtle guitar. The second incarnation was on CD1 of the twenty fifth anniversary collection, and had a thicker accordion accompaniment, with Derek's voice again. On *The Dublin Rebellion 1916* it gets the full works, with the Celtic Symphony Orchestra backing, blokeish melodious military-type singing in unison, and Noel's whistle taking centre stage in the introduction, enhanced with reverbs, the digital version of an echo chamber, the sound equivalent of being in a spotlight, some distance from the folk purity of the first version and sounding magnificent.

Another consequence of the split was the distribution of vocals to the most appropriate voices, with Brian doing his clever detailed lyrics, Noel doing the masculine marching songs, and Tommy doing the tear-jerking sentimental ones.

Brian had found inspiration in the Irish Civil War to immortalise certain events in song. There were no battles, just skirmishes, so traditionally local heroes were identified around the country. Also in the repertoire of this order are Seamus O'Duthaigh's 'Sean South of Garryowen', and 'Kevin Barry', written anonymously after he was tortured and executed, despite an international campaign for mercy, as he was so young. There is also the early recording of Brian McMahon's song about the shocking event in County Kerry in the 1920s, where there was no shortage of inspiration: 'Valley of Knockanure', with a marvellous arrangement discreetly featuring Noel. It has been said that a feature of nationalist defeat is its transformation into spiritual victory; 40,000 people turned out for the funeral of Sean South, a pious and universally admired young man.

During this time, meanwhile, the group's recording success had continued apace, notably after Bloody Sunday, with a strong theme of Irish independence, and still with Dolphin Records.

- 'On The One Road'/'Longkesh' - DOS.98 - June 1972 this went to number 20 in the Irish charts
- 'Highland Paddy'/'Give Me Your Hand' - DOS.103 - January 1973 number 19 in the charts
- 'Gloriah'/'Ireland Over All' - DOS.109 - January 1973
- 'Up and Away (Helicopter Song)'/'Ireland Over All' - DOS.112 - October 1973 Fastest selling single of all time in Ireland and number 1
- 'Michael Gaughan'- Unknown - September 1974 number 18 in the charts
- 'Rock On Rockall'/'Deportees' - DOS.123 - December 1974 went to number 17

Then a change to their own label, Triskel Records:
- 'Vale of Avoca'/'Botany Bay'- TRS.1 – 1976 [date not known]
- 'Farewell to Dublin'/'Paddy's Green Shamrock Shore' - TRS.2 - May 1976
- 'Quare Things in Dublin'/'Misty Foggy Dew' - TRS.3 – 1977
- 'Padraic Pearse'/'Ta Na La'- TRS.4 - May 1979 number 4
- 'Fourteen Men'/'The Punt' - TRS.5 - August 1979 number 19
- 'The Lough Sheelin Eviction'/'Si Beag, Si Mor'- TRS.6 – 1980

- 'Ms Fogarty's Christmas Cake'/'The Wren' [SEP] - TRS.7 - 1980
- 'Streets of New York'/'The Connaght Ranger' [SEP] - TRS.8 - May 1981 number 1
- 'Admiral William Brown'/'Cait Ni Dhuibhir' - TRS.9 - April 1982 number 4
- 'Farewell to Dublin'/'Colleen Bawn' - TRS.10 - February 1983 number 11
- 'Irish Eyes'/'Joe McDonnell' - TRS.11 - May 1983 number 3
- 'Merman'/'The Piper That Played Before Moses' - TRS.12 - November 1983 number 21
- 'Song of Liberty'/'Slainte Don A Baird' - TRS.14 - June 1984 number 2
- 'Janey Mac, I'm Nearly Forty'/'The Flower of Scotland'- TRS.15 - October 1984 number 16
- 'My Heart Is in Ireland'/'Michael Collins' MCA Records - Unknown - May 1985 number 2
- 'Dreams of Home'/'Far Away in Australia' Tara Records - TRS.16 - May 1986 number 6
- 'Remember Me At Christmas'/'Uncle Nobby's Steamboat' Triskel Records - TRS.17 - November 1986 number 7
- 'Flight of Earls'/'St Patrick's Day' Tara Records - TRS.18 - February 1987 number 1
- 'Flow Liffey Water' Triskel Records - TRS.19? – June 1988 number 6
- 'Celtic Symphony' Harmac Records - Unknown - September 1989 number 14
- 'Ireland's World Cup Symphony' Westmoor Records - Unknown - May 1990 number 12

By anybody's standards, and for whatever reason, this is remarkable success, and would not have happened without musical excellence. Unfortunately restricted by the dispute.

Pin ups now. New Spotlight August 31st 1972
(Wolfe Tones Archive)

Chapter 9

1922 onwards

'A terrible beauty is born', as post-Rising Dublin was described by the poet W. B. Yeats in 'Easter 1916'. Following the creation of the Republic of Ireland, some momentous events cemented the new nation. In 1937, the Constitution came into force, replacing the Irish Free State and creating 'Éire', or 'Ireland'. Ireland joined the United Nations in 1955 and the European Community in 1973. This was appreciated intellectually and with pride, whereas social and economic conditions impacted on the citizens on a daily basis.

The reaction to the violence of the Civil War – following on from the First World War, failures of the potato crop, evictions, disease and emigration – was a pressing economic need to increase the population and an overwhelming popular wish to restore moral values. Ireland was not in a position to give financial incentives to increase family size as other European governments did later, but the alliance of church and state achieved both. De Valera, who had moved from Sinn Féin leader to setting up Fianna Fáil, and believed in the power of capital and the ballot box, may have been influenced too by the thinking behind the Penal Laws. The recognition of the power of the church to control popular behaviour. Catholic principles were enshrined in the Constitution. Education, under Church auspices, was intended to instil discipline and obedience, concepts fundamental to the time. Just to be on the safe side, contraception was not just banned but criminalised, as of course was abortion. Anyone thinking of marrying a Protestant was contractually bound to have their children baptised Catholic. Children had to be born in wedlock, and life was made almost unbearable for young women who transgressed in the church mother and baby homes and the Magdalene laundries. It was observed that a child born in a slum stood a better chance of survival if it stayed there because medical attention was frequently denied in these homes, as was conventional burial ritual. The Bon Secours nuns ironically moved on to providing medical care to the general population subsequently. Meanwhile, the Catholic elite stepped in to re create quasi-British institutions such as the legal profession.

It has been commented that Sinn Féin had not had a plan for social reform, so did not engage the agricultural community and the desperate desire and need for land reform 'Freedom before Future' being their slogan. It was Parnell who had actually delivered the Land Commission, which changed rural life, but he was himself brought down by religious bigotry. Unionisation, which had started before the Rising, continued, and a vacuum in social policy was filled by the Catholic elites and politicians, who scented success, and united against the fear of communism, which, it was believed, appeared more attractive after the recent Russian Revolution. Social reform was resisted under this guise and the creation of a welfare state refused, in favour of religious voluntary welfare organisations, with only the relief of complete destitution considered to be a matter for the state.

Charlotte Despard had continued her humanitarian work, commenced in Nine Elms, London, with a forerunner of social services, feeding children and pregnant women at her own expense in Dublin. She made use of the status accorded by her brother Field Marshal French, later Viceroy of Ireland, and with Maud Gonne did her best to help the families of the people caught up in the politics, making fact-finding tours to places which were otherwise inaccessible, such as west Cork. Despite her wish to reconnect with her Irish ancestry, the pair of them were given the courtesy accorded to foreigners, and were both given the title 'Madame'. As mentioned before, they were known as 'Madame Charlotte Desperate' and 'Madame Maud Gonne Mad', respectively. Charlotte Despard was easily recognisable, wearing sandals and a mantilla, and word went out that she was not to be arrested, which worked until she found out and started wearing boots instead.

The Wall Street Crash had a knock-on effect that destroyed the American economy and commerce, creating unemployment on a massive scale. This led to a reduction of orders for manufacturing components from Britain. Ireland, on the other hand, remained basically agricultural, and unchanged. Emigration was to Britain instead of America, consequently. Despite the efforts of the Church to extol the virtues of clean, fresh country air, against the 'sinful' lure of the cities – especially foreign ones – large numbers remained unconvinced, and emigration at this time to Britain had a great appeal to many, compared to religious repression and subsistence farming with a large family. Edna O'Brien's early novels (banned by the church initially) document the mindset amongst young people at this time.

These policies condemned women to large families and, coincidentally, lives of drudgery and poverty. To ensure this women were banned from certain professions, and even jury service. So much for the aims of the Proclamation. Men, on the other hand, had little energy or time to think revolutionary thoughts, being preoccupied with supporting large families. The Constitution ensured that no recourse could be made to international law, unless the principles contained were permitted in the Constitution already.

This is a big problem still. This time, however, it is an Irish problem, and subject to Irish democracy, however skewed. A landmark Supreme Court ruling in the case of Crotty v. An Taoiseach, leading to the tenth amendment to the Constitution, placed Ireland in the unique position in Europe that changes to a European Union Act cannot become effective in Ireland without a plebiscite to change the Constitution.

During the Second World War, Ireland was officially neutral, although Irishmen continued to join the British Army – to either lukewarm support or hostility at home. Censorship at this time, in addition to the church censorship of matters sexual, was determinedly against anything that could be construed as propaganda. Postwar, the revelations of the Nazi concentration camps were initially disbelieved. Anti-Semitism was overlooked. The famous phrase 'England's difficulty is Ireland's opportunity' was at the forefront of minds. Much later, Derek's 'Admiral William Brown', about an Irish hero of the Argentinian navy, was promoted with a photo-opportunity with the Argentinian ambassador during the Falklands war; significantly, the song went to number 4. Good timing – although actually the result of a boyhood fascination with Argentina and its Irish diaspora.

The human condition therefore was one of survival still, and the continuing need to uproot in search of a better life and fulfilment 'Botany Bay', but not without the pain of leaving their country 'Flow Liffey Waters'. Once they got there, however, the work and the opportunities were there – but so was loneliness, homesickness 'Streets of New York', exploitation, and the need to defend themselves 'No Irish Need Apply'. Nonetheless, the Irish adapted, succeeded and prospered 'Hibernia', and were a credit to their country of destination 'John O'Brien'.

For the Wolfe Tones in the 1960s, this was when the young

boys were starting their recording careers with Fontana Records, starting with:

- 'The Spanish Lady'/'Down The Mines' - ETF 565 – 1965
- 'The Man from Mullingar'/'Down by the Liffey Side'- ETF 743 - December 1966
- 'Teddy Bear's Head'/'Jolly Ploughboy'/'Deportees'/'I Still Miss Someone' - TE.17491 - July 1967
- 'This Town Is Not Our Own'/'Come to the Bower' - Unknown – 1967
- 'Banks of the Ohio'/'The Gay Galtee Mountains' - TF.896 - January 1968

Also in 1968, they made the charts for the first time with:
- 'James Connolly'/'Hairy Eggs and Bacon' - TF.945 - June 1968 that went to number 15

followed by the change to Dolphin Records and a new manager, Oliver Barry:

- 'Uncle Nobby's Steamboat'/'God Save Ireland'- DOS.43 - June 1969

It has been said that the song 'Uncle Nobby's Steamboat' pioneered a new kind of Irish arrangement, which was copied by other bands later..

- 'Slieve Na Mon'/'7 Old Ladies' - DOS.59 – March 1970, which went to number 14

followed by:

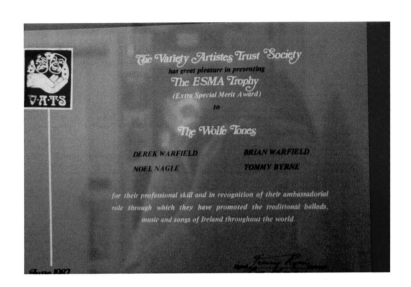

Varity Artistes Award (Wolfe Tones Archive)

Ktel award for double platinum CD sales
Wolfe Tones Greatest Hits CD 1989 (Wolfe Tones Archive)

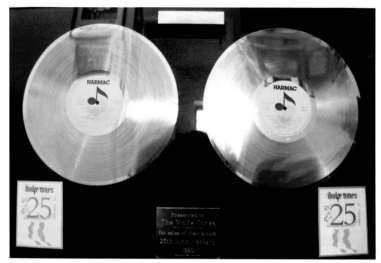

IMEG award for sales
Double Gold CD Award for Sales of 25th Anniversary CD's 1990

- 'Big Strong Man'/'Four Seasons' - **DOS.72** - **September 1970**
- 'Fiddler's Green'/'Kevin Barry' - **DOS.79** - **February 1971**

then success again:
- 'Snowy Breasted Pearl'/'Big Strong Man' - **DOS.92 - January 1972   This one went to number 7 in the Irish charts**

From 1973 onwards, the recordings, compilations, and their successes are so numerous they are best listed with their dates. They can be examined in Appendix I, and the tracks in Appendix II. It can be seen that the recording companies issuing them change from time to time.

Additionally they were presented with civic awards for their representation of Ireland and the intergrity of their personal characters. How many of their detractors and censors have received those?

*Citation for Christlike manliness in their personal and professional
lives so as to be an example to others
(Wolfe Tones Archive)*

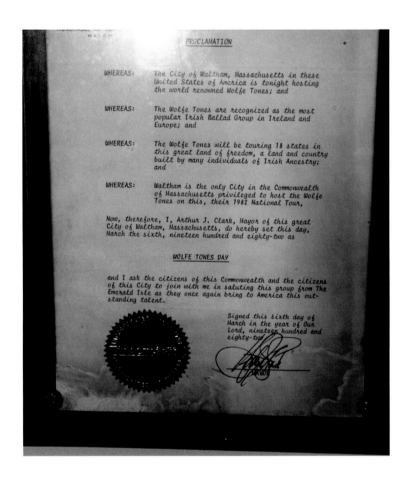

*Waltham Massachusetts Proclamation – hosting the world renowned
Wolfe Tones, the most popular folk and balland band in Ireland and
Europe...touring 18 states ... 1982 National Tour ...hereby set this day
March 6th 1982 Wolfe Tones Day*

(Wolfe Tones Archive)

Chapter 10

The North

'The only thing necessary for the triumph of evil is for good men to do nothing', said Edmund Burke, the Dublin-born statesman who moved to England and became a Whig Member of Parliament, and who supported both Catholic emancipation and the American Revolution.

Successive English monarchs had rewarded loyalty by granting Irish estates. James I had imposed a condition on those so favoured: they were required to fortify their houses and personally ensure the settling of English and Scottish Protestants in the towns, displacing Catholics in the process. The final battle signifying the end of the Gaelic era was at Kinsale in 1601, and the last of the Ulster earls left for the Continent in the so-called 'Flight of [the] Earls'. Meanwhile, the displaced indigenous Irish were made to feel inferior by the settlers and were excluded from government office because they were Catholics (in accordance with the Penal Laws).

In Ulster, Protestant opinion, led by Sir Edward Carson, feared the loss of power that would come from the creation of an Irish parliament, and in 1914 obstructed the implementation of the Liberal government's Irish Home Rule Bill, citing the war with Germany and the wisdom of conscription. Lord Randolph Churchill agreed, and secretly encouraged the creation of the Ulster Volunteer Force, supplying weapons and intelligence to them, to counter the IRA. There is a suggestion of an overlap between membership of the UVF and day-jobs in the army and the B Specials of the Royal Ulster Constabulary.

The twentieth-century Troubles were caused by the continuation of prejudice against Catholics, who were excluded from work and housing opportunities by the simple identification of their surname, and effectively excluded from the democratic process by electoral boundaries that favoured Protestant majorities. There had been violence back in 1935, prompting Charlotte Despard to move to Belfast from Dublin to assist with humanitarian projects, so it was nothing new in modern times. It was claimed that Derry (or Londonderry, to use the English name), a Catholic town, was not reached by the motorway, which terminated at Coleraine, a smaller Protestant town, financially aided to establish a university. Annual Protestant marches celebrating the Battle of the Boyne and the arrival of William of Orange were routed through Catholic areas, and were perceived as provocative. Relationships deteriorated, the civil rights movement gained momentum, and violence ensued. This was the era of Bernadette Devlin being elected to Westminster as the youngest ever MP.

Eventually, after a request from the Republic had initially been misunderstood, the Northern Ireland Assembly at Stormont was suspended by the Edward Heath government, and government functions replaced by direct rule from Westminster. The violent clashes and murders between social groups had resulted in the British army being sent as a peacekeeping force. Peace it was not. Continuing violence and the burning of Catholic homes in Protestant areas led to the tall, solid so-called peace wall being built between communities for protection. The atmosphere was oppressive; there were checkpoints and searches on main roads and at the entrances to shopping districts. Soldiers patrolled the main roads in armoured cars 'The Men Behind the Wire', and frequent searches of houses took place.

The Wolfe Tones, without labouring the point, obviously considered it a moral if not Christian duty to support the people living under these conditions, even enduring body-searches as they entered the areas. They were in effect doing in Northern Ireland, and being criticised, for what Vera Lynn, the wartime 'forces sweetheart', did in Burma to universal acclaim. Singing is a feature of religious ceremonies of all denominations for a reason – because it is believed to raise the spiritual vibrations and has an uplifting effect, and most people can recognise this 'Let the People Sing'.

The value of community singing for health is only recently being discussed, and the creation of choirs by Gareth Malone for therapeutic purposes is now being admired and televised, and displayed at concerts, such as commemorative events for soldiers killed in Iraq, for example, by the widows singing in a self-help choir. It is considered that the effort of singing, which uses the lungs more than usual, is the equivalent of active walking. Nowadays exercise is everything where health is concerned. The benefits are tangible, and measurements before and after singing practice show improvements to the immune system. Stress is known to be reduced, as measured by cortisol in the blood, and then there are the social benefits of getting together to enjoy the music. Other important releases into the bloodstream are endorphins and oxytocin, with beneficial effect, following the stimulus of music. It goes almost without saying that the music has to be of a high enough standard.

It is hard to imagine the pleasure and relief of being able to go somewhere warm and safe with your friends and family, have a drink or two, and sing along at the top of your voice with a song like 'Hibernia', with the comforting words reminding you that 'It's all right . . . we're brave resilient people', or escape to peace, in 'Ireland my Ireland'. 'In my dreams I know that I can fly', never mind how hard your life is in 'Women of Ireland' 'daughters of Erin . . . castles in the air'; 'your people enchained but you never gave in'. It must have meant so much to have an internationally successful band like the Wolfe Tones visiting you in the local community centre to remind you of the pride in being Irish, and that you were not forgotten. If you sing together a moving song about 1916 like 'Grace', so what? The effect on morale is enormous, and greatly uplifting, while the living conditions were a strain on the National Health Service. A report on health in Northern Ireland estimated that 10 percent of the adult population had regular prescriptions for antidepressants and tranquillisers. Prescribing tickets for the Wolfe Tones might have been more positive than criticising the band.

Morale, of course, is a key component of warfare. Unfortunately this was known and resented, and the Miami Showband, who were not known for the so-called rebel songs but for dance music, were massacred on 31 July 1975, which put a stop to the concerts. The subsequent enquiry showed that the decision by the Wolfe Tones not to perform in the North for some time was wise.

An article in the Belfast Telegraph on 31 July 2015 by Stuart Baillie reported that 'Amid the blackness, the talk of collusion and coverup, there is a proud realisation of the importance of music during the worst times. Stephen [Travers, a surviving band member] has no doubt about this.

'People often say that music was harmless fun. It wasn't. It must have terrified the terrorists. When people came to see us, sectarianism was left outside the door of the dancehall. They came in, they were brought together, and they enjoyed the same thing. They looked at each other and thought, there's not much difference here, and nature was doing its course.

'That's the power of music, and I think that every musician that ever stood on a stage, north of the border, during those decades, every one of them was a hero.'

Irish history has at times shared the mesmerising sense of inevitable disaster of Greek tragedy. Wanting something so much with a disappearing faint chance of legal endorsement turns hope to despair and self-destruction. This has taken the form of hunger strikes, when brave men and women have used the last resort to try to melt hard hearts or force public opinion, in order to change government policy. The suffragettes knew about this. Injustice has this effect too. The rule of law has to be upheld not just by the citizens but by the government forces too. One such hunger striker had offered words of encouragement from Brixton Prison back in the 1920s.

Terence McSwiney was the Mayor of Cork city, which had been deliberately burnt by the Black and Tans two weeks before Christmas in 1920. In total, 40 businesses (leaving 2,000 people unemployed), 130 residential properties, City Hall, and the Carnegie Library, collectively valued at £3 million (or by today's equivalent, £172 million [?€172 million]), were deliberately targeted as a reprisal for the death of one soldier and eleven others wounded earlier. The firefighters reported being shot at and having their hoses cut. Eventually it was recognised that the Auxiliaries, an aggressive force of ex-British officers attacking civilians, and also the Black and Tans, were out of control, and the British prime minister had to physically visit Ireland to call them off 'Come Out You Black and Tans'.

McSwiney had been arrested as the Commandant of the Cork brigade of the IRA. His words were later quoted by Nelson Mandela at the gates of Victor Verster prison after twenty-seven years of imprisonment: 'It is not those who can inflict the most but those who can endure the most who will succeed.'

Violence by the few against all-powerful law operating in favour of the coloniser, followed by the killing of civilians by the military, has happened on many occasions, most famously during Easter 1916. In that case, the pathologist discovered that nineteen children had died, with well-aimed bullets in their heads, out of forty under-sixteens. When Francis Sheehy Skeffington, the well-known Dublin pacifist and friend of James Joyce and Charlotte Despard, was shot summarily, it was by a military firing squad, normally reserved for military wartime deserters, even though he was a civilian. The soldiers at that time had the excuse, had they only known it, that having been engaged in the First World War, they may have been suffering from Post Traumatic Stress Disorder. Actually the officer concerned epitomised the brutality at the time, and went looking for him. It wasn't an accident, and neither were the other fifty deaths, according to Hanna, Francis's widow, in conversation with Michael Collins's chronicler. He was later court-martialled and sentenced to psychiatric detention. Normally that would be for years, but he was released after eighteen months for not being insane– and out of the army.

Pivotally for modern times, the Republic and the Wolfe Tones, civilians were killed by the army on Bloody Sunday in Derry in January 1972. This was the fourth Bloody Sunday 'Sunday Bloody Sunday' murder incident. Previously, Michael Collins 'Michael Collins' and the IRA had killed fourteen members of a British hit squad in Dublin, the Cairo Gang, after the rebellion. They had been targeting republicans during the curfew, and murdered, amongst others, the grandfather of the comedian Brendan O'Carroll, better known as Mrs Brown. The third was the same day, in retaliation, when the British army fired on the crowd in Croke Park at the final of an important championship in Gaelic football, beloved of the Volunteers. This time the situation in 1972 had arisen out of the historical prejudice against Catholics, and followed a peaceful but banned demonstration organised by the civil rights movement. It was believed that the civilians were armed; this was eventually proven to be false, but not before two enquiries – the first, with narrow terms of reference, subsequently considered a whitewash, and the second, eventually costing millions of pounds.

In the North, after the introduction of internment, the IRA had gone on the offensive and thirty soldiers died; then the army shot eleven civilians in the Ballymurphy massacre, and IRA barricades created no-go areas for the soldiers. This led to the banning of all marches in January 1972; however, two went ahead, and the 1st Parachute Regiment, noted for aggression, was sent to arrest the leaders. At the first one, rubber bullets were used. It did not transpire as intended on 30 January, when thirteen died of the twenty-six shot with live bullets. Paul McCartney's song written two days later, 'Give Ireland Back to the Irish', was banned by the BBC. The brother of a band member from the North was later beaten up. It still had international and UK chart success, despite being suppressed by the media in UK.

It was established that paratroopers had used live bullets on unarmed civilians in a peaceful demonstration protesting against the introduction of internment without trial, which had started the year before. Thirteen people were killed, including youngsters, in full view of the press. Even the advisor to Edward Heath, Lord Carrington, a distinguished soldier and senior minister, described it as 'a fairly disastrous' military operation. The language used depends on the side you support. On the one side there are freedom fighters, and on the other the upholders of law and order. The army action in 1916, in 1920, in Croke Park and in Derry, in all cases was counterproductive, and set the politically inactive population against the British. This failure may have influenced later policy not to underestimate the electorate. Actually, it is not rocket science that decent people will reject an abuse of power when a more considered approach is possible.

Internment without trial meant that anyone could be taken off the street on the slightest evidence and detained indefinitely, often for years. It was this policy that was to turn the tide in world opinion. Constant repetition of the mantra that 'we do not talk to terrorists' by Margaret Thatcher missed the point, and was just focusing on the violent effect of dissatisfaction, and not the societal inbalances causing it, as O'Brien points out [in Political Censorship in Modern Democracy in bibliography]. Not widely known at the time was that Mrs Thatcher had had plans/feasibility studies prepared at the same time as for those for the Channel Tunnel to construct two tunnels to Ireland from Britain one between Wales and the Republic and the other between Scotland and Northern Ireland as well as another to France for cars. These exist still, of course, for "an ever closer union."

Those who actually were members of the IRA wanted political status, which was denied them, and they were treated like criminals. In 1976, convicted paramilitary prisoners were denied Special Category Status, which led to the Blanket Protest, because they refused to wear prison uniforms. This followed the example of Seán McCaughey from County Tyrone. When his death occurred in Portlaoise Prison in May 1946, he had served four years in solitary confinement, two clothed only in a blanket. Over the next five years the situation deteriorated in full view of the world, and a number of men who had gone on hunger strike started to die. One of them was Joe McDonnell 'Joe McDonnell'. The ballad, written by Brian in his role of balladeer commenting on current events, creates a powerful moment in the concerts, when sung by Tommy. Many people believe that this is the most enduring of the songs written during this sad period in Irish history.

Tommy preparing to sing Joe McDonnell Easter 2016

The support by the Wolfe Tones was the start of criticism of the band, and their songs, simply because of the politics of the North. Vested interests choose to interpret songs purely about 1916 as if they apply to 1976. The only thing that links them is the patriotic desire to unify Ireland. Modern liberal thinking is that colonialism is bad and patriotism is good. We understand colonialism as the occupation of one country by another, usually for commercial reasons. This may be initiated by force because of the resistance of the native population, even if it is not necessarily maintained by force. In the twenty-first century, it may be deemed old fashioned because of the greater access by the multinational companies for the same purpose. Patriotism is the love of an individual for the country of their birth, and the desire to preserve its culture, history and customs from dilution or coercion.

The Irish Republican Army of 1916 evolved and split over the next sixty years several times, through political changes and internal disagreements, into something very different, and so did its methods and the circumstances. Rifles used and evoked romantically in song 'Rifles of the IRA' were replaced through several stages to Semtex in the 1970s – which has nothing to do with the Wolfe Tones. Eventually the IRA organisation was decommissioned and disbanded, after the people of Northern Ireland finally got the diplomatic solution that resolved the conflict, in the form of the Good Friday Agreement, with the assistance of Senator George Mitchell from Maine. This does not dilute the desire to reunite Ireland, which persists, in line with Freudian and Kleinian theory, outlined by Bion [bibliography]. The idea is that in times of persistent dispute, a small part of the group holds a watching brief, staying true, freeing the rest to carry on, pending a final resolution which is acceptable to all. In Ireland's case, this applied to the factions of the IRA but has mistakenly been applied to the population as a whole, with consequences for the administration of the Republic. The treatment of the Wolfe Tones will be shown to have been considered collateral damage. The situation is much more complicated than a simple vote can resolve.

One thing is sure: the nature of the debate changed when Ireland joined the EU, because European law is supreme over national law. No longer does the coloniser have the last word. There is the European Court of Justice to arbitrate; similarly, all citizens can apply directly to the European Court of Human Rights if they believe their rights have been breached, such as the right to a fair trial (Article 6) or free speech (Article 10). The compatibility of any judgment with the Irish Constitution is something to be examined and resolved by the lawyers, and it is argued that this is the arena of future dispute, rendering weapons and bloodshed obsolete. This was the strategy followed by the RTÉ journalists. Preventing warfare between nations was the reason for the creation of the European institutions in the first place, after the Second World War.

The terms used to describe all these events and their associated powerful emotions again vary, according to the side you are on. One man's freedom fighter is another man's terrorist such as men like Nelson Mandela and Martin McGuinness, both of whom became respected statesmen politicians. Folk music takes snapshots of life in different eras quite simply, but where politics are concerned, inferences are subtly conveyed by the terms chosen. It is not just deliberately pejorative associations with English words, which was to follow the introduction of Section 31 of the Broadcasting Act in the Republic. A feature of colonialism is the suppression of native language, which historically was undertaken to facilitate trade and administration in the language of the invader. It may have been described as the need to communicate with modern society, such as the suppression by force of the Breton language and the imposition of French as the dominant language. Likewise in Cameroon, one colonial language (English) was suppressed by another (French). The teaching of Irish is a past and current issue, with a subtext of independence and the suppression of a culture 'As

Gaeilge'.

An enduring mystery is why patriotic people who want to serve their country as a political representative [TD] in the Republic should, once elected, become hostile to the wishes of many people to unify Ireland, which is a historical, heartfelt goal. Logically, a lengthy rolling programme leading to support for this goal could have avoided much bloodshed, even if nothing were to follow. So the question must be asked about what politicians learn when they join the government that convinces them so firmly not to support this. A clue may lie in the cost to Britain of administering Northern Ireland.

'According to Oxford Economics, in the financial year 2006/07 Northern Ireland paid £11.5 billion into the national accounts and received £18.7 billion out, for a net "cost" of £7.2 billion to the rest of the UK' (May 21st 2016, www.quora.com). In addition to the elevated cost of health services, unlike Wales and Scotland there is no tax income available to central government, but a deficit of more than £7 billion. Also, the local economy is supported by one in three people working for the government, to ease the burden of unemployment.

The British treasury applies formulae to calculate the grants available to devolved administrations, such as the Barnet formula, but recognises that actual need must be assessed to override this. Taking this instead in 1979, and the figure 100 per capita as the baseline for England, the calculations are Wales 109, Scotland 116 and Northern Ireland 131.

Conversely, there is a considerable reliance on trade with Britain to support the economy of the Republic. 'Britain is far and away Ireland's biggest trading partner, accounting for 50 percent of exports from the Republic. Ireland is virtually entirely dependent upon its larger neighbour for energy, importing 90 percent of its oil and more than 90 percent of its gas from the UK . . . trade barriers would jack up prices of Irish imports from the UK. The effect on the Republic could be devastating' (Chris Blackhurst, *Independent,* 13 February 2016). The *Journal* on 15th April 2015 had a similar point of view: 'we currently export 16 percent of manufactured goods and 19 percent of services to the UK, with imports totalling 34 percent and 18 percent respectively. Given the barriers that will arise if Britain becomes a non-EU territory, the impact on our trade would be significant.'

This was the position, then, after the benefit of the European fund's boost to the economy [Celtic Tiger], the financial crash and the recovery, as well as the benefits of offering preferential rates of corporation tax. It was even more important then in earlier times not to fall out with Britain.

If this ended abruptly in response not just to Brexit but to mass support, either violently or through the ballot box, the economy of the Republic would be devastated, according to these figures. Far from eventually affording social policies on a par with Britain, such as a free-at-the-point-of-delivery National Health Service, which must influence even the least forceful in Northern Ireland, everyone would suffer – or so it would appear. This idealistic aspiration could be a poisoned chalice if it was translated into a practical reality now, on the basis of these figures. It is purely a question of timing and economic development, therefore, and not something that any career politician would wish to admit.

One has, however. 'Fine Gael candidate for Dublin Brian Hayes has called Northern Ireland an "economic wasteland" (*www.the journal.ie*, 9 May 2014).

Not everybody takes this pessimistic view, however. Things will change, adding another dimension, post-Brexit, for Britain, and when Northern Ireland becomes free, in 2017, to vary its own corporation tax, because all three administrations will compete to use this rate to attract inward investment. In fact, administratively speaking, there are reasons for Britain to be willing to divest itself of Ulster, and others for the Republic not to want to take it on without payment. This conflicts with the accepted view.

More recently, it has been postulated by Meagher [bibliography] that unification is inevitable, because of the operation of the markets, and international agreements, and quite peacefully and apolitically. So much pain could have been avoided if the responsibility had been taken to use RTÉ to educate and inform of the distinction between idealism, albeit achievable, and pragmatic economic reality.

A commissioned economic study in Canada takes the view: that Ireland as a whole could actually benefit from unification, in both the short term and, ultimately, the long term, via the adoption of the euro and tax harmonisation with the Republic. It analyses three possible scenarios in which Britain and the Republic share the cost while dependence on British administrative employment is gradually reduced, and employment shifts as prospects improve, with appropriate education for the markets, and inward investment. Denigration of this study has started already, with an inference of bias by those taking an opposing idealistic view, but the point is that increasing economic advantage, not idealism, will provide the impetus for change.

During this period, the Wolfe Tones continued to release CDs, many of which were re-releases.

Of the few new releases were two collaborations with a young band, the High Kings, one a charity single, and the other as guests on their CD (see Appendices), which are interesting. They were both recordings with Celtic Collections; the association of youth and fame must be mutually beneficial, but also illustrates a feature of the Irish music scene. The careers of the Wolfe Tones were mapped out from an early age because of family support and general support for Irish cultural activities. Some of the High Kings' band members were the children from the Irish music dynasties the Fureys and the Clancys, both well known to the Wolfe Tones.

Brian also supported two of his children in their musical activities with appearances alongside the Wolfe Tones, including publicity in the CD insert for the *Dublin Rebellion 1916* CD, favoured over Tommy and Noel, at the three-day residential celebration. This demonstrates that the nepotism that can bring down politicians is an essential apprenticeship process for musicians in this tradition. It is logical that the children of certain professions, such as doctors and actors – for most activities, in fact – need to observe and understand the constraints of success, and benefit from the close training of skills. It may seem unfair to the jealous, but it makes for excellence.

*Promotional photo for Gleneagles with the Fureys: From front left is
Johnny McEvoy, George Furey, Paul Furey , ??, Derek Warfield,
Eddie Furey, Back: Dermot O'Brien, Tommy Byrne and Maurice
O'Donoghue, Owner of the Gleneagles Hotel Killarney, two unknown
ladies, some unnamed boys and two Irish Draught horses
(Wolfe Tones Archive)*

The Wolfe Tones sing of the history of Ireland out of love for Ireland and the Irish people, and the traditional desire for 'freedom'. That's all. In so far as they express a desire for a new Ireland to be administered by one Irish government, they are only reflecting the historical idealism of the documented bulk of the peaceful population. Commenting on their political appeal, Derek said, 'When we recorded in London, an article for MCA compared our singing to the resistance singers in Central and South America. We really filled a very important vacuum of resistance, and when evaluated by history it is very important that we kept alive that resistance through music. It is more important than our personal differences.'

It has not been made known, because of the deliberate sidelining of their careers, but the astonishing truth is that they were instrumental in bringing about the diplomatic solution to the protracted pain that was life in the North since the partition of Ireland, which was needed all along.

A PhD thesis by Glasgow university student Alan Stuart Macleod concludes that it was fear of the Irish-American grass roots in America, not an intergovernmental request, that ultimately brought Senator Mitchell to intercede in the talks which resulted in the Good Friday Peace Agreement in 1998. He was particularly well qualified, being half Arab himself, and a highly experienced diplomat, having worked with the Israeli Palestinian conflict. It came about because the Irish-American diaspora are so keen to hear tales of the privations that brought their ancestors to America. Having had twenty-two top-twenty hits and platinum albums over the years is one part of the evidence that the Wolfe Tones delivered consistent musical excellence, which caused them to be in demand the length and breadth of America alone, and which continues after 54 years at the time of writing. They combined this with many discreet charity fund-raising activities, such as raising money for children's holidays, St Patrick's Day parades, and medical support.

	1916 SYMPHONY ON TOUR	
HAPPY ST PATRICKS DAY TO ALL		
Thursday 2nd March 2017	Carneys Bar & Grill, 136, Broadway Ave, Amytiville, N. Y. 11701	Tickets and Info 1 631 464 4445
Friday 3rd March 2017	Sweeney's Irish Pub. 33. Orange Ave. Walden, N.Y. 12586	Tickets & Info 1 845 778 3337 & 1 845 591 7274
Saturday 4th March 2017	New Point Comfort Fire Station, 192, Carr St. Keansburg.N.J.07734	Tickets & Info Call Bill, 1 732 670 4974. Email wmk007748@aol.com
Sunday March 5th 2017	Monaghans, 48, Nth Village Ave, Rockville Center, N.Y.11570	Tickets & Info 1 516 318 5948
Wed Mar 8th	Molly's Maguire's, 1085,. Central Ave,. Clark, N J. 07066.	Thix & Info 1 732 388 6511.
Thursday March 9th	AOH Hibernian Hall. 2. Wellingotn Ave. Newport, R.I.02840	1 401 847 8671 & 1 860 214 9302 & 1 401 225 9696
Friday March 10th	Shandon Court, 115, East Main St, Islip, N.Y.11730	Info 1 631 7862994
Sat March 11th	IBEW. BOSTON 256. Freeport St. Dorchester. MA 2122	Info 1 617 436 5150
Sunday March 12th 2017	Shanahans Bar & Grill, 515, Old Dock Rd, Kings Park. N Y 11754.	Tickets & Info 1 631 921 3304 .
Wednesday March 15th	Connollys Bar & Grill. 121, West 45th St, N.Y.10036	Info 1 212 587 5129

Touring Schedule now - a brief snapshot of the intensity and pressure still from wolfetonesofficialsite.com

Appreciative audiences initiated the presentation of illuminated addresses signed by civic and state dignitaries testifying to their musical excellence – in Ohio, Boston and Kansas City, to name but three – in which they are described as ambassadors for Ireland. A feature of the American civic and state process is the proclamations issued to bring attention or recognition to a person, group or cause. Through a proclamation, the governor or mayor may announce policy and declare a feature of collective thinking. They may even designate a day, week or month for commemoration. This is influential in its creation and when made widely known certainly at the moment of presentation, and if subsequently reported. Some of these documents are entered in the Executive Journal an administrative ledger. They cannot fail to have a persuasive effect on the electorate and hence other politicians, more importantly. The Wolfe Tones have been presented with several to date including one extolling their moral character. The band has also had at least two designated Wolfe Tones Days for the days they performed. The quality of the performance, the duration of their careers and the impressively researched subject-matter of their songs are the subject of the proclamations. The songs about coffin ships and emigration for work 'Botany Bay', the heartfelt desire for independence, and yes, hunger strike, in 1981, had the effect of raising consciousness and in the end summoning the cavalry 'Thank God For America'.

Another consequence of their popularity and the respect in which they are held is that they were presented with the keys to not just New York but also Los Angeles.

The Wolfe Tones with Mayor Lindsay of New York and Sergeant Pearse Meagher founder of the NYPD pipe band on the occasion of the award of the keys of New York, demonstrating the political influence from the grassroots of Irish America.(Wolfe Tones Archive)

A remarkable statement by Carroll Hughes, a Wolfe Tones fan in Rhode Island and a member of the Ancient Order of Hibernians [AOH], explains exactly how it came about:

'I have been seeing the Tones since 1985. As a lobbyist working at the legislature in Hartford I always brought numbers of legislators to the concerts. They in turn brought proclamations recognising their role in bringing attention to the Troubles. The thing occurred in March, when we had them at the AOH in Newport. In this case the Mayor presented a resolution. No song did more than 'Joe McDonnell' to bring attention to the cause. It's a little like a very patriotic song. The room is quiet; we all know the words; Tommy adds the passion. Between 'The Town I Knew So Well' (Coulter) and 'Joe McDonnell', everyone had a feel for the Troubles.'

Following the appointment of Senator Mitchell, the net result, after considerable discussion, was the Good Friday Agreement or Belfast Agreement, signed on 10 April 1998, which dramatically improved things. The pen really is more powerful than the sword.

So there you have it. It is difficult to think of greater achievement. The word 'success' seems trivial by comparison. The power of song indeed.

Pat Boone with Wolf Tones in America.

The Los Angeles 'Rose' Deirdre O'Reilly.

The Bearded Ones
★ ★ ★

get keys of city

THE bearded ones . . . the Wolf Tones . . . scored a Beatle-sized hit in the U.S.A. . . . they are still basking in the sunshine of their own reflected glory even thought they are now back on the "Ould sod" delighting fans in the provinces.

D. J. Curtin, lead of Kerry Blues playing at A.G.S. Olympic Wednesday.

STAR DUST

According to manager Oliver Barry the tour was a blending of Irish hearts and Irish song for on many occasions the audience joined lustily with the patriotic choruses.

The grand finale of a tour which included Irish clubs and halls from Frisco to Ensenada down Mexico way took place at Los Angles where they had to run the gauntlet of fans and were eventually smuggled on to the plane.

Between-the-show highlights included a real "Irish night" at Blarney Castle a swanky Los Angeles night spot where the bearded Minstrels were invited to step forward and choose the little lady who would represent the city in the "Rose of Tralee" finals next month. Their choice received a storm of applause when 19-year-old, blond and blushing Deirdre O'Reilly, the winner, stepped forward to take her bow before a crowd of well nigh 2,000.

Biggest thrill came when Mayor Yorty, who had earlier made the Wolfe Tones honorary members of his Sister Cities Committee (Los Angeles and Dublin) presented them with the keys to the city. The first musicians since the Beatles to receive the honour.

Dermot O'Brien and his Clubmen playing Jetland tonight.

DERMOT'S NEW L.P.

PLAYING to night in Jetland, Limerick, is the popular Dermot O'Brien and the Clubmen. Keeping faith with his fans, Dermot, Co. Louth exGaelic fotball star and musician supremo, turned down an offer to take the band to South Africa. "Too many home dates," said Dermot. Everyone

is waiting for the band's forthcoming disc release. Four tracks are already on tape in the Eamonn Andrews Studios, and when time permits several more will be run. This will be an L.P. (name to come) and will be followed by a single when a choice has been decided on.

Keys of Los Angeles (Wolfe Tones Archive)

CITATION of RECOGNITION

WHEREAS, The Ancient Order of Hibernians and The Shamrock Club of Columbus are devoted to the promotion of Irish history and culture in the Greater Columbus area, and are honored to bring The Wolfe Tones to Columbus to celebrate Irish Heritage and the memory of St. Patrick; and

WHEREAS, The Wolfe Tones are the Republic of Ireland's premier international vocal group, weaving tales of Irish myth, legend and history through story, lyric and song; and

WHEREAS, the City of Columbus is honored to have The Wolfe Tones make Columbus a regular stopping point during their annual tour of the United States during the St. Patrick's Day season and recognizes The Wolfe Tones' role in many contributions promoting and encouraging the goal of a unified and peaceful Ireland:

NOW, THEREFORE, I, Gregory S. Lashutka, Mayor of the City of Columbus, Ohio, do hereby issue this Citation of Recognition to:

THE WOLFE TONES

and urge all members of our community to join in recognition of this significant occasion and the achievements above mentioned.

IN WITNESS WHEREOF, I have hereunto set my hand and caused the Great Seal of the Mayor of the City of Columbus, Ohio, to be hereto affixed this _____ day of February, 1997.

_____

Gregory S. Lashutka
Mayor

Proclamation Columbus Ohio, extolling the remarkable qualities of the Wolfe Tones and the desire for a unified and peaceful Ireland, initiated by the Ancient Order of Hibernians. (Wolfe Tones Archive)

Chapter 11

Irish Broadcasting

It is ironic that for the Wolfe Tones, a lifetime earning a living singing about Irish history should risk being curtailed by Irish history itself.

After Bloody Sunday 'Sunday Bloody Sunday', as it became known in Derry/Londonderry, on 30 January 1972, feelings ran so high in the Republic that two days later, 50,000 people marched in Dublin in protest, culminating in the burning of the British embassy. They had previously burned down British Home Stores. This was before the lies, decorations to the soldiers concerned, and parliamentary cover-up, when Bernadette Devlin was prevented, against constitutional convention, from giving her account of what had happened to Parliament.

In 1974, Dublin and Monaghan saw car bombs set off on the same day; relatives of the 33 dead and 300 injured victims believed the crimes were not fully investigated. In 1993, the Ulster Volunteer Force admitted responsibility. Two good reasons for the Irish to be profoundly angry, if they knew the true facts. The UVF had been created by Sir Edward Carson at Churchill's suggestion, armed by the British army, supported by British intelligence, and later subsumed into the B-Specials of the Northern Irish Police Force, specifically to counter the IRA. The enquiry into the shooting of the Miami Showband revealed that this association with members of the Ulster Defence Regiment (UDR) was also then in force, having been banned and then permitted, in order to include them in the peace talks.

The Irish government in the Republic held a debate in 1976, in which Conor Cruise O'Brien spoke. O'Brien advocated restriction of free speech where it was likely to 'play on the emotions, through words and images, in ways likely to arouse fear and hatred, to cause acute distress, or to endanger the lives of citizens, and the security of the state responsible for those lives. . . . but its actual working should be exposed to continued scrutiny and to renewed debate, so as to ensure that a restriction accepted for the protection of the citizens is not abused for the exclusive benefit of their rulers'.

The result of the vote was that free speech was officially curtailed by the Broadcasting Authority (Amendment) Act, 1976, which redefined Section 31 of the Broadcasting Act, 1960. Shades of the Defence of the Realm Act of 1914, except that this was introduced by an Irish government which was not at war with anyone. The new provision required that the ministerial order be renewed or withdrawn by the Oireachtas every year. It removed the power of the Minister responsible for broadcasting to sack the RTÉ Authority, as had been done previously.

A study in 1978 conducted by the Economic and Social Research Institute found that a clear majority rejected IRA activities, and also that a clear majority supported self-determination for the entire island of Ireland. Following publication, it must be assumed that it was believed that neutrality could be swayed by republican manipulation. These people, the 'nonviolent' electorate wanting a united Ireland, were deemed by the continued annual renewal of the provision therefore to be unstable, and to need to be shielded from any facts and figures that might convince them otherwise, and tip them over into violence. It was implied that the truth could anger them and that debate would not deflect the anger but lead to violence. It could also be interpreted that the facts and figures that persuaded people to want a united Ireland simply by voting for it were dangerous. The unspoken fear could have been the mind-blowing idea that a vote in the Republic could vote in favour of unification without any violence at all. What would be the economic and political implications of this embodiment of the Greek principle of democracy?

The ancient Greeks gave us two concepts: democracy and catharsis. Catharsis is the belief that expressing a strong emotion in a way that deflects its harm is beneficial and effective in reducing the strength of the emotion. That if you are furious, hitting a punch bag will get rid of the temper and stop you hitting the person responsible. Various studies have shown that this is a myth. It is better not to express anger at all but to think of something else. So angry debate does not dissipate anger.

Democracy, on the other hand, is the way they controlled the population. The idea is that if everyone eligible thinks they have a fair and equal say in how they are governed, they will accept the laws that are created. Modern democracy relies on the principles of informed consent, so that full knowledge is available about the candidates: their characters, their opinions, and the nature of the tasks of government they will have to deal with. The economy, for example: something that makes most people's eyes glaze over unless they are likely to be made redundant.

The assumptions are breathtaking: for example, that a TV interrogation of political candidates could make a law-abiding person become themselves physically violent. What are the facts and figures that are so dangerous? What must the electorate be prevented from finding out? What do the politicians know that would make them introduce draconian powers? It need not be out of tyranny, but paternalism. Could it possibly be tales of torture and deliberate threats of harm to the public and the economy?

The Heath government had been advised by Lord Carrington, the defence secretary, a man with considerable gravitas. The longest-serving minister, who had been awarded the military cross in a distinguished military career, he would be difficult to ignore if you were a weak, inexperienced politician. Brian Faulkner was to indicate that he had been responsible for the introduction of torture in the North. If a politician does not want to go down in history as losing a national 'asset', and asks a military man for advice, he cannot complain if he gets a military response involving weapons and soldiers. It was to be a long time before they came up with a diplomatic solution instead.

Minister Jim Mitchell had quoted the Supreme Court judgement which highlighted that 'a democratic State has a clear and bounden duty to protect its citizens and its institutions from those who seek to replace law and order by force and anarchy, and the democratic process by the dictates of the few'. Except that the Republic was not apparently the target, apart from the UVF car bombs, nor its citizens, and the democratic process was being controlled by the few.

Conor Cruise O'Brien had set out his thinking in a speech which was considered well crafted at the time, that reads like the conclusion was written before the reasons, in which he argued that it was reasonable to suppress information in these circumstances in the way that one would support the suppression of crime, and that an eloquent exposition of moral argument, fact and philosophy could lead to harm.

Just a moment. Can you really equate suppression of free

speech and suppression of crime? Prevention of crime requires clear drafting of the criminal law so that no one is in any doubt. Harmful speech could more clearly be identified by specific instances, surely? Race-relations legislation, for example, where everyone knows where they are? Broadly phrased legislation is too open to biased interpretation: like, for example, assuming that singing traditional Irish songs can make people violent. This is like criminalising the singing of Davey Crockett or the fifties theme to the TV series Robin Hood. Both historic figures known to have killed for their countries so both technically rebel songs in this provocative categorisation of songs about folk heroes.

The strategy was described by Mark O'Brien as a silencing project to make citizens and media professionals wary of expressing a contrary opinion, for fear of sanction or public hostility. At the same time, this would tend to amplify the party-line analysis of the situation. He said the consequence was that 'asphyxiating silence' characterised the Southern response to the Northern conflict.

The net result was that broadcasting anyone involved with Sinn Féin or the IRA was banned. This went further, it was argued by Mark O'Brien, as a process of marginalising these opinions in their different forms: mockery, for example. This generally made these opinions less acceptable to the wider population. Ironically, as it would become apparent that this would include singing 'A Nation Once Again'.

As Niall Meehan wrote in the *Sunday Business Post* on 20 April 2003: 'Under cover of Section 31 of the Broadcasting Act, RTÉ had systematically extended the scope of the censorship order. It had prevented a Sinn Féin member (now Sinn Féin councillor) Larry O'Toole from speaking about a trade union dispute in which he 4was the spokesperson. After the High Court declared the practice illegal, RTÉ appealed to be re-censored and told the Supreme Court it "would not allow a Sinn Féin actor to advertise a bar of soap". The US Newspaper Guild declared: "We are astonished that RTÉ, instead of welcoming this liberal interpretation of an abhorrent censorship statute, is asking the Irish Supreme Court for a greater restriction of its free-speech rights.'"

RTÉ said that its blanket ban was an exercise of its discretionary powers. Yet when faced with precisely the same dilemma, the BBC said that a Sinn Féin member could not be held to be representing his or her party during every waking moment. Under British censorship rules, Gerry Adams was broadcast speaking on behalf of constituents. Since the 1970s, RTÉ had been ordered to stop Sinn Féin and IRA representatives or spokespersons from being broadcast. Section 31 permitted governments to issue an annual censorship order. Loyalists were also banned, but by common admission of Ministers, Section 31 was aimed at Sinn Féin.

The order issued by Fianna Fáil Minister Gerry Collins in 1971 led to the sacking of the RTÉ Authority and the jailing of journalist Kevin O'Kelly over his refusal to name IRA chief of staff Sean MacStiofain as the voice on a taped interview. After Conor Cruise O'Brien became Minister for Posts and Telegraphs in 1973, he accused RTÉ of allowing a 'spiritual occupation' by the IRA. A new management regime was put in place. Those who would not toe the line were sent to agriculture, children's and religious broadcasting.

By 1976, the National Union of Journalists said that the government line on 'security' issues was not questioned by RTÉ. There were major stories of local, national and arguably world significance that RTÉ was afraid to touch."

As a consequence, RTÉ could not interview or question Sinn Féin politicians or supporters, even (or especially) prior to elections.

For middle managers and presenters, the choice was clear: go along with it or risk being sacked. Not something wanted on a CV if you harbour ambitions to work for the BBC, a huge British international organisation with many opportunities for promotion, glory and now a golden future in Salford. This is a well-worn path for the employees of RTÉ, such as Eamonn Andrews and Terry Wogan. It includes the BBC World Service, which by a coincidence conducted a poll in 2002 to find the best single of all time; from a number of international finalists, the winner was 'A Nation Once Again', written by Thomas Osborne Davis in the 1840s, and the version recorded by the Wolfe Tones!

For journalists, however, the restrictions were particularly serious, because their role is to assist the public by questioning high-flown assertions and grounding the debate with facts and figures and highlighting inconsistencies: in other words, the very process the legislation was designed to prevent. As Ireland is a member of the EU, its citizens have the right to European justice, in this case the right of direct access to the European Court of Human Rights, which enforces the rights incorporated into national law described by the European Convention of Human Rights. Of particular relevance in this context is the right to free speech under Article 10.

The journalists felt so strongly about the gagging of their questions for politicians that they decided to challenge it at the ECHR. A case was eventually heard: Purcell v. An Taoiseach. They lost. The reason given was the association of Sinn Féin with the IRA. This decision could be a factor in the later decision to decommission and disband the IRA. Legislation such as Article 10 appears to offer so much, but the crude statement of the right is accompanied by subclauses of exceptions to the principle. This is where the idea of the greatest good to the greatest number offers an exception with a choice of criteria, in this case on the grounds of maintaining public order. Less contentious issues can be lost in domestic court cases for practical reasons, such as, if granted, they would open the floodgates to others, and the court system would be swamped, or they would cost too much; these criteria are open to interpretation by judges.

Betty Purcell, who was the producer at RTE who brought the case after other attempts to change things failed, later wrote a book about the RTE experience and quoted Cezanne" ...paint it as it is" and commented "a true artist refuses to be swayed by the regard of a patron, or the political fallout of a piece of work. He/she attempts to get to the truth about what is represented. And therein lies the attraction." Writing of October 1976 and the time of Conor Cruise O'Brien/Liam Cosgrave, in an aside she wrote "Northern Ireland as a political entity was not recognised by the government of the Republic at that time; yet the British Administration in Northern Ireland was given the power to decide who could and could not be interviewed on RTE's airwaves." The atmosphere was oppressive, heads rolled and the search for Sinn Fein members to exclude went to such lengths as to seriously impede the ability of RTE journalists to interview in all contexts not just the political.

So one must not be too harsh in criticising RTÉ for not booking the Wolfe Tones, however unjust, and not for being enemies of the state but for having an influence over the majority of the law-abiding electorate. It is very unsatisfactory when middle managers make decisions in back rooms instead of in the open, denying the opportunity to prepare a defence to known charges, with evidence and witnesses. Following the wholesale replacement of the board of RTE and the working practices described by Betty Purcell one might presume a bias against the wish for a united Ireland by the replacements.

Of course a simpler explanation might be wanting to forcefully stop the animosity towards Britain in the wake of Bloody Sunday, and to prevent the truth of the Dublin bombings and the Miami Showband Massacre becoming widely known, while the possibility of two tunnels between Britain and Ireland were under consideration. The lethal pollution of Beaufort's Dyke in the sea and the lack of commercial cost effectiveness put the Scottish link on hold. The Welsh one is still under consideration. At £60m per kilometre the favoured route is Dublin Holyhead but was deemed to be of more benefit to Ireland who would have to pay half, too difficult financially. Forcibly ignoring history past and present, however, doesn't make it go away.

By being licensed by the Broadcasting Act to perform the government function of broadcasting, RTÉ is technically an 'emanation of the state' under European law, and so is subject to the same administrative law as government departments. This means that judicial review is possible if any of a number of criteria are met, such as demonstrating bias, unfairness or error. RTÉ was also set up in the same way as the BBC, to educate, inform and entertain.

When the evidence is clear, often the department concerned

carries on as if it had been found guilty without waiting for a court hearing, and reconsiders its decision anyway, because this is the best result possible for a successful hearing. The court cannot order a change of decision.

It is therefore interesting to speculate that when the Wolfe Tones were unexpectedly invited by RTÉ to a televised studio discussion in 2002, after a long absence from the airwaves, and no doubt as a result of correspondence from thousands of people wanting to see them, it could have been as a token reconsideration of the decision, or wishing to be seen to comply with the founding principles. It failed on the first count because the Wolfe Tones had only themselves to respond, on the hoof, to unfair criticisms without evidence or representation. It failed on the second because it was one-sided and took the criticisms out of context.

Their accuser, an elegant essayist, was encouraged to feel confident enough to assertively attack their manner of earning a living in front of millions of people on the basis of his own 'personal opinion' and meagre 'evidence' from just one line from each of two of Brian's songs. Mainly it was based on one line of the song 'Celtic Symphony', which had been commissioned for the centenary of Glasgow Celtic Football Club – a subject very dear to Warfield hearts – and taken from the esoteric graffiti around the pitch. Short, catchy, and a gift to a songwriter: 'Oo ah, up the 'RA'. This personalised inclusion was tailor-made to comply with the specific brief.

The other concerned one line in 'Rock on Rockall' about disputed ownership of an island in Irish territorial water retained by the British with a connection with oil and gas resources, with the line 'Burn your arse and blow yourself to hell' offering contemptuous advice on what they, that is the

British, can do with it. Creatively phrased the way it was, it could have been paraphrased as 'Stick it up your arse and go to hell'. This was not an instruction as to what Irish people should do to them.

The point failed to be made of the many legitimate links between composers and football chants and songs; associations such as Shostakovich with Zenit Leningrad, Elgar and Wolverhampton Wanderers, Tony Britten commissioned to pen the UEFA Champions League Anthem and here Brian Warfield with Glasgow Celtic.

Identified Ulster journalists were in the audience, specially invited for the purpose thus rendering the scenario one sided, although one critic, from the South, spoke of why they felt uncomfortable being in a place they would never have chosen to attend anyway: a Wolfe Tones concert. The discussion was therefore slanted, with the goal of influencing public opinion in the way observed by Mark O'Brien: to make certain points of view unacceptable and to undermine the influence of the Wolfe Tones. It failed to uphold the founding principles because it did not educate or inform about the context of the government propaganda intention, and it failed to entertain because they were expected to talk and not entertain in the way their TV-licence-holding fans wanted, and had endorsed enough over the years to create twenty-two Irish top twenty hits. Bias, in other words.

A pity the band members were kept in the dark about the real issues. On the other hand, did the presenter and the guests know? Did they believe they were entertaining the public by criticising the band in this way? It failed the propaganda test, however, as indicated by an overwhelming vote for the Wolfe Tones by the representatives of the law-abiding electorate present in the studio and others too, later on in the phone in, demonstrating their enduring views at the same time in a vote. The programme was actually a back-handed compliment to the band, demonstrating a belief in their influence and popularity.

They were to appear on TV again a couple of times, but without the distinction being made about their support for the martyrs of 1916 having been confused with the bombs prior to the peace agreement. Throughout this period, the part other volunteer groups in the North, including the UVF, played in the violent past has never been emphasised.

Another aspect of all this is that showbusiness goes hand in hand with the publicity industry. Casual viewing of TV talent contests demonstrates just why it is called 'the oxygen of publicity', and just how much being seen on TV can influence public opinion, and ultimately sales. Even if it only creates one-hit wonders, being without it makes the success of the Wolfe Tones all the more remarkable. It also introduces the possibility of a sinister intention to harm their career, or at least a callous disregard for the effect on it, quite apart from hoping to reduce their influence on the general population. Knowing this those wanting a united Ireland as soon as possible naturally embrace the Wolfe Tones as their own. The Wolfe Tones cannot be blamed for ensuring they are entertained accordingly, because they can then be sure of continuing to work, having been cut off from the mainstream in this way. Not quite the intended effect.
The success of the Wolfe Tones was attributable to other factors too obviously. As Derek said 'A lot of our success was due to the chosen material and the makeup of the band. That blend was unique. As a unit of four it worked very well. Success has many fathers failure is an orphan!"

The Sinn Féin broadcast ban was lifted in 1993 as part of the Peace Process. Section 31 specifically was not renewed by Senator later President O'Higgins nor was it repealed.

An appearance on German TV where they were not so constrained
(WolfeTonesTV)

Chapter 12

Conclusions and Celebrations

Once the political events of the last fifty years have been examined, the success of the Wolfe Tones is all the more remarkable. The politicians don't come out of this well; in fact, their actions demonstrate an anxiety so serious that it can cause the abuse of the airwaves. One can suggest alternative strategies that might have avoided the apparent kneejerk reactions, but even then we cannot know yet just what external pressures they might have faced. History may deliver the explanation. The rationale behind Section 31 is reminiscent of a riddle on UK TV, when viewers were asked to picture a scenario where a plane crashed across a national boundary, with one wing in one country and the other in the neighbouring country. The question was: 'In what country would the survivors be buried?' After various attempts to answer, it eventually became clear that the answer was 'In neither', because survivors are not buried. Similarly the fact that the majority of the Irish electorate is against violence should not indicate instability and a need for strict censorship. If it was a question perhaps of if they should learn they were still at serious physical risk of terrorist attack the entire scenario might have been seen differently.

Reviewing Irish history, it is staggering that we ourselves have lived through a time when singing about Ireland must not be broadcast, and not wanting to share control of the island of Ireland must not be discussed, and stories of heroes who tried to change things have been deliberately dismissed. This situation is not dissimilar to past centuries, in fact. Most surprising is that in an age of mass education, political insight, universal suffrage and belief in democracy, not to mention the internet, certain political ideas and practices had to be suppressed. Eventually, of course, Senator O'Higgins acknowledged these very factors in his article in the O'Brien book [bibliog.] It is hard to believe this strategy was devised by Irish people who grew up believing that such political censorship was wrong in antiquity. It was so strange that perhaps the authors of the law change were not educated in Ireland? The subsequent public award of honours in a violent scenario can only add insult to deliberate humiliation, so pointlessly as to be malign and incredible.

Despite Section 31 no longer being renewed the Wolfe Tones are still missing from the media, such as largely being eliminated from reports of big events or historical contributions to traditions. The assistance they provided with fundraising efforts over a period of years, and the failure to report Derek's appearances at the White House, and later outside the GPO at

Easter 2016 are examples of this. The disparaging of any nationalist sentiment has done its work ostensibly. Of course they have been at it for half a century and are not the next new thing but they have achieved as much as the masters of the entertainment industry whose every minor action is feted in the press.

Dublin Centenary at City West with the Celtic Symphony Orchestra.

It is not fanciful to imagine that without the Wolfe Tones touring the world and performing the traditional balladeer role of 'telling it how it is', things could be very different. Without the diplomatic solution to perceived injustice, we could still be on the carousel of military 'solutions', and be witnessing attempts for yet another Anglo-Irish Treaty, after even more Bloody Sundays. What they have done in effect is complete a comprehensive campaign for hearts and minds of 54 years duration to date, and they are still at it. In fact, they have been at it longer than all the politicians (apart from Sinn Féin, perhaps). Tommy said at one point in their documentary that at the height of their fame, they were touring for eleven months of the year. Now that is a public-information initiative! It could not have been achieved if the music had not seduced and the well researched lyrics resonated with the family history of the descendants of the survivors of Irish tragedy.

The irony of the situation has almost a poetic justice and religious symmetry or, as James Connolly might put it, the Marxist dialectic. The more their message was suppressed and their career opportunities restricted, the more defiant the content of their programme became, and as a direct consequence of the attempt to suppress their careers in Ireland and the need to earn a living, the more important it seemed to carry on, where they could. In the entire world! And they did. Significantly, it was, at last, in the context of talk of justice and decommissioning that they were free to decide to take different musical directions.

Certainly the experience of the Wolfe Tones explains the lack of Irish music played as a percentage of airtime. Once this is considered, the historico-political flavour to the lyrics of many of the songs of other bands becomes apparent as a possible factor in its absence from the airwaves. Even U2, with a different style of music, felt the need to make a point of prefacing one of their songs by saying: 'This is not a rebel song.' However, discovering that Wikipedia had a completely misleading definition of those songs for some time suggests an explanation for the bias. It makes the apparent freedom of speech of other countries rare and wonderful.

There is a concerted effort by current Irish musicians to change the composition of music playlists presently. They make the point that other nations require broadcasters to include a certain percentage of national music, and would like the same to be done in Ireland. Forty years after Bloody Sunday, the politics are different, so perhaps this might happen.

The moral of this story for those – the majority of people in the Republic – who want Ireland to be united by peaceful means, seems to be to encourage their children to learn law, not just domestic but public, constitutional and European, because at last the debate is where it should be. The others must work to ensure that the economy may be able to offer social policies that match anything people in the North receive at present. The major inequities in the North have been identified and addressed. The place to concentrate on now is the Republic. It is just a shame that during those years, the people who placed their trust solely in RTÉ for news, insight and entertainment were denied political analysis when it mattered, and a rich musical experience.

Ireland is an island. All of it. This is indisputable. Everything else on a daily basis is a series of administrative tasks, onerous or otherwise. Thankfully, there is no longer a need to die for Ireland because not only are there legal processes to invoke, but Ireland needs everyone alive to help. In the event that Ulster were to wish to share its administration with the Republic, despite the interference of European politicians concerned with the Brexit negotiations, one could argue for a dowry from Britain in view of the disproportionate costs – a similar conclusion to the models tested in the Canadian commissioned study [bibliog]. However, a detailed analysis of Ireland's financial position, both nationally and within international contexts, now gives hope to many. There is now a strongly held belief that the island may inevitably have a consensual unified administration achieved through international economic and political forces – and, what's more, would benefit from it.

Ireland has benefited greatly from the Wolfe Tones' success, despite government obstructiveness and lack of gratitude. They have contributed in spades, not just financially but in terms of well-being and national pride. They have been presented with modern illuminated addresses in the form of proclamations from American civic and state dignitaries that confirm their success as ambassadors for their country. During their careers, the band members have celebrated various milestones with anniversary CDs and special concerts.

Following the Irish practice of staging concerts in large hotels has enabled fans from all over the world to enjoy the residential experience and attend several concerts consecutively, each with a different theme. The centenary of the Republic was such an experience, and the Wolfe Tones pulled out all the stops, with an orchestra and a marching band on the first night alone. Such is the success of the recorded repertoire and the longevity of the band that, remarkably, the entire audience knows every word of every song, and joins in freely. One night is not enough to go through the favourites. Even the students, who can only have heard the songs from their parents' collections, know the words. This is in Ireland, before we even begin to consider the rest of the world.

It was staggering how many nationalities were present at City West over three nights. They knew, being mainly of Irish descent, how important an occasion it was. As the concerts marked the centenary of the events leading to the creation of the Republic, they were momentous enough, but after 54 years of performing songs articulating the pride in the bravery of the heroes of 1916 and the idealism for the unification of Ireland in the future, it was particularly important for the Wolfe Tones.

*Students Dublin 2017 - word perfect and enjoying themselves,
although none of them born when Streets of New York was at number
One*

After 54 years they've still got it... and the wild student enthusiasm!

The Celtic Symphony Orchestra celebrate the Centenary in Dublin, here accompanying Tommy's solo

The songs were performed in the uniform of the Volunteers, with the full Celtic Symphony Orchestra in Dublin (where else?), over the three nights of Easter 2016.

This was the venue to experience the full force of Brian's musical vision, and the drama and power were breathtaking. It was interesting for fans of long duration and some intensity to compare the musical evolution of the band. Powerful as it undoubtedly was, it epitomised the contrast with the purist folk vision. Regardless of your position, it has to be acknowledged that these arrangements permit great individuality but still retain the folk character of the early days. The trouble with the strict traditional interpretation is that it is just that. Aiming for a purist loyalty must show less individuality – or so I thought, before listening to Derek's *Far Away in Australia* CD. Let us not forget, however, the full range of beautiful non political songs, covering the gamut of human experience and emotion, that has been an enduring part of their repertoire. Commemorative CDs and DVDs were released of the centenary three nights of concerts, as had been throughout the 54 years performing history of the band, at the twenty-five-, forty- and fifty-year anniversaries – all remarkable milestones, and enthusiastically received.

Later during the centenary year, on 1 May in Dublin City Hall, they performed 'A Nation Once Again' below the gaze of Thomas Osborne Davis, Young Ireland himself, the writer of this patriotic song. The audience were given copies of the *Dublin Rebellion 1916* CD with the new songs, whilst raising funds for a Dublin charity. Once again, everyone knew all the words. It was a historic moment of great pride for all.
Make the most of them while you can.

Thomas Osborne Davis looks down with shared pride on A Nation Once Again *at Dublin City Hall 2016*

Appendix I

Recordings

from www.theballadeer.com

1965-1974

- The Foggy Dew: 1965 - Fontana TL5244 LP (mono)
- alt: The Foggy Dew: 1965 - Fontana STL5244 LP (stereo) — slight track variation
- Up The Rebels: 1966 - Fontana TL5338 LP
- The Rights of Man: 1968 - Fontana TL5462 LP
- Rifles of the IRA: 1969 - Dolphin DOL 1002 LP
- Let The People Sing: 1972 - Dolphin DOL 1004 LP
- Till Ireland A Nation: 1974 - Dolphin DOL 1006 LP

1975-1989

- Irish To The Core: 1976 - Triskel TRL 1001 LP
- Across The Broad Atlantic: 1976 - Triskel TRL 1002 LP
- Belts Of The Celts: 1978 - Triskel TRL 1003 LP
- As Gaeilge: 1980 - Triskel TRL 1004 LP
- Live alive-oh!: 1980 - Triskel TRL 1005 (2) LP
- Spirit of the Nation: 1981 - Triskel TRL 1006 LP
- A Sense Of Freedom: 1983 - Triskel TRL 1012 LP
- Profile: 1985 - MCA WTLP 1 LP
- Sing Out For Ireland: 1987 - Triskel TRL 1015 LP
- 25th Anniversary: 1989 - HMCD 50 LP CD

2001-

- You'll Never Beat The Irish: 2001 - Celtic Collections TRCD 015 CD
- The Very Best of Wolfe Tones Live: 2002 - Celtic Collections CCCD 300 CD
- re: ... Special 40thAnniversary Edition: 2005 - Celtic Collections CCD 040 CD

- w/Five additional songs
- Rebels and Heroes: 2003 - Celtic Collections CCCD 635 CD
- The Troubles: 2004 - Celtic Collections TRCD 020 CD
- :Celtic Symphony 2006 - Celtic Collections CCCD 023 CD
  Child Of Destiny: 2012 - Dolphin DOLTVCD128 CD
  The Dublin Rebellion 1916: 2016 - Rebel Records   CD

EP & Single releases
- 1960's
- **Spanish Lady&Down the Mines: 1965 - Fontana TF 565**
- **Man From Mullingar&Down By The Liffey Side: 1966 - Fontana TF 743**
- **This Town Is Not Our Own& Come To The Bower: 1967 - Fontana TF 804**
- **Teddy Bear's Head: 1967 - Fontana TE 17491 EP**
- **Banks Of The Ohio&The Gay Galtee Mountains: 1968 - Fontana TF 896**
- **James Connolly&Hairy Eggs and Bacon: 1968 - Fontana ETF 945**
- **Uncle Nobby's Steamboat&God Save Ireland: 1969 - Dolphin DOS 43**

1970s
- **Slievenamon&Seven Old Ladies: 1970 - Dolphin DOS 59**
- **Big Strong Man & The Four Seasons: 1970 - Dolphin DOS 72**
- **Fiddlers Green & Kevin Barry: 1971 - Dolphin DOS 79**
- **Snowy Breasted Pearl & Big Strong Man: 1972 - Dolphin DOS 92**
- **On The One Road&Long Kesh: 1972 - Dolphin DOS 98**
- **Highland Paddy & Give Me Your Hand: 1972 - Dolphin DOS 103**
- **Ireland Overall & Gloria or Glorieh [sic]: 1973 - Dolphin DOS 109**

- Up & Away (The Helicopter Song)&Broad Black Brimmer: 1973 - Dolphin DOS 112
- Rock On Rockall & Deportees: 1975 - Dolphin DOS 123
- Botany Bay & Vale of Avoca: 1978 - Triskel TRS 1 [?]
- Farewell to Dublin & Paddy's Green Shamrock Shore: 1979 - Triskel TRS 2
- Padriac Pearse & Ta Na La: 1979 - Triskel TRS 4
- Fourteen Men & The Punt: 1979 - Triskel TRS 5

1980-1985
- The Lough Sheelin Eviction & Si Beag, Si Mor: 1980 - Triskel TRS 6
- Miss Fogarty's Christmas Cake & The Wren: 1980 - Triskel TRS 7
- Streets Of New York & Connaught Ranger: 1981 - Triskel TRS 8
- Admiral William Brown & Cait Ni Dhuibhir: 1982 - Triskel TRS 9
- Farewell To Dublin: 1983 - Triskel TRS 10
- Irish Eyes & Joe McDonnell: 1983 - Triskel TRS 11
- Merman& The Piper that played before Moses: 1983 - Triskel TRS 12
- Song for Liberty & Slainte Don A Baird: 1984 - Triskel TRS 14
- Janey Mac Im Nearly 40& Flower of Scotland: 1983 - Triskel TRS 15
- My Heart Is In Ireland& Michael Collins: 1985 - Triskel/MCA WTS1
- My Heart Is In Ireland & Toor A Loo: 1985 - MCA 1003

1986-1990
- Dreams of Home & Far Away In Australia: 1986 - Triskel TRS 16
- Remember Me At Christmas & Uncle Nobby's Steamboat: 1986 - Triskel TRS 17
- Flight Of Earls & St. Patrick's Day: 1987 - Triskel TRS 18

- I Love Wolfe Tones: 1988 - Triskel TREP 1 EP
- Christmas With The Wolfe Tones: 1988 - Triskel TREP 2 EP
- Flow Liffey Water: 1988 - Triskel TRS [?]
- Celtic Symphony: 1989 - Harmac [?]
- Ireland's World Cup Symphony: 1990 – Westmoor

- 2001-
- Song for World Cup 2002: 2002 - Celtic Collections CCSCD 2002 CD/EP
- A Nation Once Again - 21st Century: 2003 - Celtic Collections (single release
- On The One Road: 2010 (Charity single)— w/The High Kings

Compilation Recordings
1970-1990
- Teddy Bears Head: 1971 - Dolphin DOLM 5005 LP
- Golden Irish Ballads –Volume One: 1984 - Dolphin DOCX 9007 CASS
- Golden Irish Ballads –Volume Two: 1984 - Dolphin DOCX 9008 CASS
- Greatest Hits: 1986 - K-Tel records ONE 1326 LP
- Very Best of The Wolfe Tones: 1999 - Celtic Collections CTCCD012 CD
-
2000-
- Millennium Celebration: 2000 - Celtic Collections TRCD2000 CD
- Greatest Hits: 2000 - TARA PXNARCD002
- Greatest Hits: 2000 — Erin/Valley Entertainment ERIN 15087 (& Valley VE 15087) CD
- 20 Golden Irish Ballads –Volume One: 2002 - Dolphin DOCDX 9007 CD

- 20 Golden Irish Ballads –Volume Two: 2002 - Dolphin DOCDX 9008 CD
- Golden Irish Ballads – Volumes One & Two: 2005 - Dolphin WT2CD1 CD
- Both Volumes of the above "20 Golden Irish Ballads".
- 50 Great Irish Rebel Songs: 2005 - Dolphin DWWT3CD1 CD
- as "Derek Warfield & The Wolfe Tones"
- 1916 Remembered: 2006 - Celtic Collections CCCD 1916 CD
- The Platinum Collection: 2006 - EMI (?) CD
- The Anthology Of Irish Song: 2008 - Celtic Collections CCCD 050 CD

Guest Appearances—The High Kings— w/The Wolfe Tones[1]
- On The One Road: 2010 (Charity single)
- Memory Lane: 2010 - Universal 2732558 CD

Anthologies (Selected)[2]
- Folk in Focus: 1968 - Fontana FJL 505 LP
- Folk Favourites: 1970 - Contour 6870 636 LP
- A Feast Of Irish Folk: 1977 - Polydor 2475 605 LP
- Another Feast of Irish Folk: 1980 - Polydor EYETV1 LP
- KILMAINHAM Jail - It's heroes and songs: 1980 - Dolphin DOLM5026 LP
- Thousands Are Sailing: 1999 - Shanachie 78025 CD

Re-releases

Up The Rebels
- 1970 - Dolphin DOLM 5003 LP
- 2002 - Dolphin DOCDX 9023 CD

Rifles of the IRA
- 1971 - Cynda CNS 1008 LP— (Canadian release)
- 1971 - Kelenn 6332 627 LP— (French release)
- 1971 - Metronome MLP 15.498 LP— (German release)
- 1991 - Shanachie SH 52030 CD

·   2001 - Triskel TRCD010 CD

Let The People Sing
·   1972 - Boot BOS-7117 LP— (Canadian release)
·   1972 - Metronome 201.047 LP— (German release)
·   1982 - Triskel TRL 1007 LP
·   1991 - Shanachie SH 52031 CD
·   2001 - Celtic Collections TRCD005 CD

Till Ireland a Nation
·   1983 - Triskel TRL 1011 LP
·   2001 - Celtic Collections TRCD009 CD
·   200(?) - Triskel TRCD 1011 CD

Irish to the Core
·   1976 - Triskel TRL 1001 LP
·   1993 - Shanachie SHA 52033 CD
·   2003 - Celtic Collections EICD628 CD

Across the Broad Atlantic
·   1993 - Shanachie SHA 52032 CD
·   2001 - Celtic Collections TRCD006 CD
·   2009 - Spirit EICD 627 CD

Belt of the Celts
·   1978 - Triskel TRL 1003 LP
·   1993 - Shanachie SHA 52035 CD
·   2000 - Celtic Collections TRMCD012 CD
·   2003 - Spirit EICD629 CD

As Gaeilge
·   2001 - Celtic Collections TRCD 014 CD
·   2003 - Spirit EICD631 CD
      ·

Live Alive Oh
·   1992 - Shanachie SHA 52029 CD
·   2001 - Celtic Collections TRCD004 CD

Spirit of the Nation
·   1991 - Shanachie SHA 52028 CD
·   2001 - Celtic Collections TRCD002 CD

A Sense of Freedom
·   1992 - Shanachie SHA 52026 CD
·   2001 - Celtic Collections TRCD007 CD

Profile
> 1992 -Shanachie SHA 52027 CD
·   2001 - Celtic Collections TRCD003 CD

Sing Out for Ireland
·   1993 - Shanachie SHA 52034 CD
·   2001 - Celtic Collections TRCD008 CD

25th Anniversary
·   1991 - Shanachie SHA 52024 CD
·   2001 - Celtic Collections TRCD001 CD

Child of Destiny
> 2012 - Dolphin Records B0069CLPVQ CD

The Dublin Rebellion 1916
> 2016 - Rebel Records   CD

Appendix II
The tracks and where to find them

Year	Album Details	Track Listing	Peak Chart Position Ireland
1965	The Foggy Dew Format: LP Label: Fontana Records (TL5244)	1.The Singing Game 2.Down in the Mines 3.Dicey Reilly 4.Galway Races 5. Louse House in Kilkenny 6. The Diamond 7. The Zoological Gardens 8. The Foggy Dew (Rev. C. O'Neill) 9. The Peeler and the Goat (D. Ryan) 10. The Sash 11. Limerick Rake 12. Dry Land Sailors 13. Follow Me Up to Carlow (P. McCall) 14. The Hills of Glenswilly 15. The Boys of Wexford (P. McCall/A. Darley) 16. Roisin Dubh	—
1966	Up the Rebels Format: LP Label: Fontana Records (TL5338)	1. The Man from Mullingar 2. Tri Colored Ribbon 3. The Dying Rebel 4. Finding Moses 5. Banna Strand 6. Banks of the Ohio (R. Patterson) 7. Down by the Liffey Side 8. The Valley of Knockanure (B. MacMahon) 9. Blow Ye Winds 10. The Black Ribbon Band 11. The Old Maid 12. Goodbye Mrs. Durkin 13. Song of the Backwoods	—
1968	The Rights Of Man	1. The Rights of Man	—

		2. Raynard the Fox
	Format: LP Label: Fontana Records (TL5462)	3. Long Black Veil (D. Dill/M. Wilkin) 4. Up the Border 5. A Rover 6. Ode to Biddy McGee 7. Wrap the Green Flag Around Me 8. Enniskillen Fusilier 9. Treat Me Daughter Kindly 10. Four Strong Winds (I. Tyson) 11. The Banks of the Sweet Smirla Side 12. Lagan Love
1969	Rifles of the I.R.A. Format: LP Label: Dolphin Records (DOL1002)	1. Slievenamon 2. Erin Go Braugh 3. God Save Ireland (T. Sullivan) 4. The Sun is Burning (Ian Campbell) 5. Big Strong Man 6. In Garran na Bhile 7. Four Seasons 8. Rifles of the I.R.A. 9. Skibbereen (P. Carpenter) 10. Sweet Carnlough Bay 11. Ships in Full Sail 12. Sean Tracy (Tipperary So Far Away) 13. Holy Ground 14. Uncle Nobby's Steamboat	—
1972	Let The People Sing Format: LP Label: Dolphin Records (DOL1004)	1. The Snowy-Breasted Pearl 2. Sean South of Garryowen 3. Twice Daily 4. James Connolly 5. Don't Stop Me Now 6. Taim in Arrears 7. Come Out Ye Black and Tans (D. Behan) 8. On the One Road 9. The Men Behind the Wire (P. McGuigan) 10. For Ireland, I'd Not Tell Her Name	—

Year	Album	Tracks	
		11. Paddy Lie Back 12. First of May (B, R & M Gibb) 13. Long Kesh 14. A Nation Once Again (T. Davis)	
1974	'Till Ireland a Nation Format: LP Label: Dolphin Records (DOL1006)	1. Highland Paddy 2. Traveling Doctor's Shop 3. My Green Valleys 4. The Boys of the Old Brigade 5. Children of Fear 6. The Boys of Fair Hill 7. The Bodenstown Churchyard (T. Davis) 8. The Grandfather 9. The Blackbird of Sweet Avondale 10. Broad Black Brimmer 11. Laugh and the World Laughs with You 12. A Soldier's Life 13. Give Me Your Hand (R. O Cathain) 14. Must Ireland Divided Be 15. Ireland Over All	—
1976	Irish to the Core Format: LP Label: Triskel Records (TRL1001)	1. Botany Bay (P. Stephens/W. Yardley/F. Pascal) 2. The Water is Wide 3. The Irish Brigade 4. Graine Mhaoil 5. Whelan's Frolics 6. The Night Before Larry was Stretched (W. Maher) 7. Fiddler's Green (J. Connolly) 8. The Vale of Avoca 9. The Limerick Races 10. The Jackets Green 11. The Cook in the Kitchen and the Rambling Pitchfork 12. Kevin Barry 13. Rock on Rockall	—
1976	Across the Broad Atlantic Format: LP	1. The Rambling Irishman 2. Paddy on the Railway 3. The Great Hunger	—

	Label: Triskel Records (TRL1002)	4. Many Young Men of Twenty 5. Sweet Tralee 6. Shores of America 7. A Dream of Liberty (S. McCarthy) 8. Paddy's Green Shamrock Shore 9. Goodbye Mick 10. Spancil Hill (M. Considine) 11. The Fighting 69th 12. The Boston Burglar 13. Farewell to Dublin
1978	Belt of the Celts Format: LP Label: Triskel Records (TRL1003)	1. Misty Foggy Dew 2. Quare Things in Dublin 3. The Fairy Hills 4. Connaught Rangers 5. Bold Robert Emmet 6. The Hare in the Heather 7. Ta Na La 8. Some Say the Devil is Dead 9. General Munroe 10. Hurlers March 11. The West's Asleep 12. The Boys of Barr na Sraide 13. The Rose of Mooncoin 14. Rory O'Moore	—
1980	As Gaeilge Format: LP Label: Triskel Records (TRL1004)	1. Caoine Cill Cáis 2. Sí Finn 3. Amhrán Na Breac 4. Thugamar Féin An Samhradh Linn 5. Brabazons 6. Cáit Ní Dhuibhir 7. Cuan Bhantraí 8. Rosc Catha Na Mumhan 9. I Ngarán na Bhfile 10. Éamonn an Cnoic 11. Siún Ní Dhuibhir 12. Tá na Lá 13. Reels 14. An Dórd Feinne	—
1981	Spirit of the Nation Format: LP Label: Triskel	1. Dingle Bay 2. No Irish Need Apply 3. Down by the Glenside	—

	Records (TRL1006)	4. Bold Fenian Men 5. Paddle Your Own Canoe 6. Padriac Pearse 7. The Lough Sheelin Eviction 8. Song of the Celts 9. Butterfly 10. Protestant Men 11. Only Our Rivers Run Free 12. St. Patrick was a Gentleman 13. Ireland Unfree 14. Carolan's Concerto 15. Streets of New York (Liam Reilly)	
1983	A Sense of Freedom Format: LP Label: Triskel Records (TRL1012)	1. Merman 2. Sgt. William Bailey 3. Farewell to Dublin 4. Adm. William Brown 5. Catalpa 6. Irish Eyes 7. Flower of Scotland 8. Michael Collins 9. Slainte Dana no Baird/Cailin O Chois tSiuire Me/Planxty McGuire 10. Galtee Mountain Boy 11. The Piper that Played Before Moses 12. Let the People Sing 13. Joe McDonnell	—
1985	Profile Format: LP Label: MCA (WTLP1)	1. My Heart is in Ireland 2. Wearing of the Green 3. Mullingar Feadh 4. Plastic Bullets 5. Macushla Mavoureen 6. Song of Liberty 7. Women of Ireland 8. Butcher's Apron 9. Little Jimmy Murphy 10. The Sailor St. Brendan 11. Toor a Loo Tooralay 12. Far Away in Australia	—
1987	Sing Out for Ireland Format: LP	1. Flight of Earls Liam Reilly 2. Croppy Boy	—

	Label: Triskel Records (TRL1015)	3. The Impartial Police Force 4. Janey Mac, I'm Nearly Forty 5. Carolan's Favorite 6. The Guilford Four 7. Annabell 8. St. Patrick's Day 9. Radio Toor-I-La-Ay 10. Paddy's Night Out 11. Great Fenian Ram 12. Bonny Mary of Argyle 13. Kiss the Old Mother, Hug the Old Man 14. A Soldier's Song	
1989	25th Anniversary Format: CD Label: Shanachie Records {SHA52024}	CD One 1. Celtic Symphony 2. Merry Ploughboy 3. Women of Ireland 4. Rock on Rockall 5. The Foggy Dew 6. James Connolly 7. The Man From Mullingar 8. Flow Liffy Waters 9. First of May 10. The Piper That Played Before Moses 11. The Big Strong Man 12. Janie I'm Nearly Forty 13. Give Me Your Hand 14. The Boys of the Old Brigade 15. Dingle Bay 16. Monsignor Horan CD Two 1. Boston Rose Liam Reilly 2. The Zoological Gardens 3. The Broad Black Brimmer 4. Newgrange (Bru Na Boinne) Derek 5. Treat Me Daughter Kindly 6. Come Out Ye Black and Tans 7. Slieve Na Mban 8. Far Away in Australia 9. Goodbye 10. Helicopter Song 11. Oro Se Do Bhatha Abhaile	Gold

		12. The Merman 13. The Teddy Bears Head 14. Banna Stand 15. Many Young Men of Twenty 16. The Wests' Awake	
2001	You'll Never Beat the Irish Format: CD Label: Celtic Collections (TRCD015)	1. You'll Never Beat the Irish, Part 1 2. The Crossing 3. The Rebel 4. In Belfast 5. Chicago 6. We are the Irish 7. United Men 8. Ireland My Ireland 9. Halloween 10. Grace 11. The Hot Asphalt 12. Thank God for America 13. Celtic Dreams 14. You'll Never Beat the Irish, Part 2	—
2004	The Troubles Format: CD Label: Celtic Collections (TRCD020)	Disc One: 1. This is the Day 2. The Patriot Game (D. Behan) 3. The Song of Partition 4. Children of Fear 5. Sunday Bloody Sunday (J. Lennon) 6. Plastic Bullets 7. The Men Behind the Wire 8. Lough Sheelin Eviction 9. Go Home, British Soldiers 10. Danny Boy (F. Weatherly) 11. Star of the County Down 12. In Belfast 13. Up the Border 14. The Green Glens of Antrim 15. The Old Orange Flute 16. The Old Brigade (Dance Medley) Disc Two: 1. Lament for the Lost 2. We Shall Overcome	41

		3. You'll Never Beat the Irish, Part 3 4. Tyrone 5. Must Ireland Divided Be 6. Song of Liberty 7. The Orange and the Green 8. Long Kesh 9. The Sash Me Father Wore 10. Fermanagh Love Song 11. Hills of Glenswilly 12. Joe McDonnell 13. County of Armagh 14. Gildford Four 15. Billy Reid 16. Up the Rebels (Dance Mix)
2012	Child of Destiny Format: CD Label: Dolphin Records (B0069CLPVQ)	1. Child Of Destiny 2. Swing A Banker 3. The Cliffs Of Moher 4. Hibernia 5. Uncle Nobby's Streamboat 6. Siobhan 7. Anne Devlin 8. Moonbeams 9. The Celtic People 10. My Green Valleys 11. John O'Brien 12. Champions Of Champions 13. The Merman 14. The First Of May 15. Big Brother 16. Who Fears To Speak Of '98 17. Admiral William Brown
2016	The Dublin Rebellion 2016 Format: CD Label: Rebel Records	1. The Proclamation 2. Lonely Banna Strand 3. The Road to the Rising 4. Women of Ireland 5. Padraic Pearse 6. Grace 7. Tri Coloured Ribbon 8. Last Moments (Light a Penny Candle) 9. Wrap the Green Flag round me Boys

10.	The Rebellion
11.	Margaret Skinnider
12.	James Connolly
13.	The One Road
14.	Ireland Unfree Shall Never Be At Peace
15.	The Foggy Dew
16.	The Dying Rebel

Live albums

Year	Album Details		Peak Chart Position Ireland
1980	Live Alive-Oh! Format: Label: Triskel Records (1005(2))	LP	—
2002	The Very Best of the Wolfe Tones Live Format: CD Label: Celtic Collections (CCCD300)		20
2004	40th Anniversary Live Format: CD Label: Celtic Collections (CCDVD040)		—

Compilation albums[edit]

Year	Album Details	Peak Chart Position Ireland
1971	The Teddy Bear's Head Format: LP Label: Dolphin Records(DOLM5005)	—
1984	20 Golden Irish Ballads Format: Cassette Label: Dolphin (DOCX9007)	—
2000	Millennium Celebration Format: CD Label: Celtic Collections (TRCD2000)	—
2003	Rebels & Heroes Format: CD Label: Celtic Collections (CCCD635)	7 Double Platinum
2006	Celtic Symphony Format: CD	—

Year	Album Details	Peak Chart Position
	Label: Celtic Collections (CCCD023)	
2006	1916: The Easter Rising Format: CD Label: Celtic Collections (CCCD1916)	—
2006	The Platinum Collection Format: CD Label: EMI	35
2008	The Anthology of Irish Song Format: CD Label: Celtic Collections (CCCD050)	20

Extended plays[edit]

Year	Album Details	Track Listing	Peak Chart Position Ireland
1967	The Teddy Bear's Head Format: EP Label: Fontana Records (TE17491)	1. The Teddy Bear's Head 2. Deportees 3. The Merry Ploughboy 4. I Still Miss Someone	—
1988	I Love the Wolfe Tones Format: EP Label: Triskel Records (TREP1)	1. Flow Liffey Waters 2. Flight of the Earls 3. Newgrange 4. My Heart is in Ireland	—
1988	Christmas with the Wolfe Tones Format: EP Label: Triskel Records (TREP2)	1. Remember Me at Christmas 2. A Song of Liberty 3. Mrs. Fogarty's Christmas Cake 4. The Wren	—

Singles[edit]

Year	Title	Peak Chart Position Ireland[2]
1965	Side A: Spanish Lady Side B: Down the Mines	—
1966	Side A: The Man from Mullingar Side B: Down by the Liffey Side	—
1967	Side A: This Town is Not Our Own	—

	Side B: Come to the Bower	
1967	Side A: The Banks of the Ohio Side B: The Gay Galtee Mountains	—
1967	Side A: James Connolly Side B: Hairy Eggs and Bacon	15
1969	Side A: God Save Ireland Side B: Uncle Nobby's Steamboat	—
1970	Side A: Slievenamon Side B: Seven Old Ladies	14
1970	Side A: Big Strong Man Side B: The Four Seasons	—
1971	Side A: Fiddlers Green Side B: Kevin Barry	—
1972	Side A: The Snowy-Breasted Pearl Side B: Big Strong Man	7
1972	Side A: On the One Road Side B: Long Kesh	20
1972	Side A: Highland Paddy Side B: Give Me Your Hand	19
1973	Side A: Ireland Over All Side B: Gloria or Glorieh	—
1973	Side A: The Helicopter Song Side B: Broad Black Brimmer	1
1974	Michael Gaghan	18
1975	Side A: Rock on Rockall Side B: Deportees	17
1978	Side A: Botany Bay Side B: Vale of Avoca	—
1979	Side A: Farewell to Dublin Side B: Paddy's Green Shamrock Shore	—
1979	Side A: Padriac Pearse Side B: Ta Na La	4
1979	Fourteen Men	19
1980	Side A: The Lough Sheelin Eviction Side B: Si Beag, Si Mor	—
1980	Side A: Ms. Fogarty's Christmas Cake Side B: The Wren	—
1981	Side A: Streets of New York	1

	Side B: The Connaught Rangers	
1982	Side A: Admiral William Brown Side B: Cait Ni Dhuibhir	4
1983	Farewell to Dublin	11
1983	Side A: Irish Eyes Side B: Joe McDonnell	3
1983	Side A: Merman Side B: The Piper that Played Before Moses	21
1983	Side A: Janey Mac, I'm Nearly Forty Side B: The Flower of Scotland	16
1984	Side A: Song for Liberty Side B: Slainte Don A Baird	2
1985	Side A: My Heart is in Ireland Side B: Michael Collins	—
1985	Side A: My Heart is in Ireland Side B: Toor A Loo	2
1986	Side A: Dreams of Home Side B: Far Away in Australia	6
1986	Side A: Remember Me at Christmas Side B: Uncle Nobby's Steamboat	7
1987	Side A: Flight of the Earls Side B: St. Patrick's Day	1
1988	Flow Liffey Water	6
1989	Celtic Symphony	14
1990	Ireland's World Cup Symphony	12
2002	You'll Never Beat the Irish	19
2003	A Nation Once Again	15

Appendix III

The Wolfe Tones DVDs

Live Concerts
25th Anniversary DVD & CD
50th Anniversary DVD & 2CD
Child of Destiny boxed set DVD & CD
Let the People Sing - The Wolfe Tones Story DVD
Into the Light – 1916 Commemoration Concert Live 4 CDs 2 DVDs

www.wolfetonesofficialsite.com for merchandising details

Appendix IV

Derek Warfield
Recordings
from: www.theballadeer.com
and The Young Wolfe Tones

Original releases
Legacy: 1995 Shanachie S52042 CD
Liberte '98: 1990 Shanachie S52046 CD
Sons of Erin: 2000 Cill Dara DWLCD002 CD
Take Me Home to Mayo: 2002 Kells Music KM7014CD
    •   re: Slan Abhaile: 2005 Cill Dara DWLCD005 CD
Clear the Wayy (FaughaBallagh): 2002 KellsMusic KM7015 CD
    •   re: FaughaBallagh (Clear the Way): 2003 Cill Dara DWLCD004 CD
    •   re: FaughaBallagh (Clear the Way): 2010 CD Baby/Derek Warfield CD
A Nation Once Again: 2003 Kells Music KM7020 CD
The Bonnie Blue Flag: 2004 Cill Dara DWLCD003 CD
Songs for the Bhoys: 2005 Dolphin TORC BHOYTV2CD1 CD
    •   re: Green, White & Essential Gold Vol. 1: 2009 Dolphin DW2CD100 CD
More Songs For The Bhoys: 2005 Dolphin TORC BHOYTV2CD2 CD
    •   re: Green, White & Essential Gold Vol.2: 2009 Dolphin DW2CD101 CD
The Night Is ... Young: 2008 KELLS7148 CD — "Derek Warfield and the Young Wolfe Tones"
    •   re: On the One Road: 2009 CD Baby/Ceol Music CD — with 5 bonus tracks.
On The One Road 2009 CD002 Warfield Music "Derek Warfield & The Young Wolfe Tones"
Far Away in Australia: 2011 CD Baby/Derek Warfield CD "Derek Warfield and the Young Wolfe Tones"

Washington's Irish: 2011 CD Baby/Derek Warfield CD

Let Ye All Be Irish Tonight CD005 "Derek Warfield & The Young Wolfe Tones: Warfield Music 2013

The Call Of Erin Derek Warfield & The Young Wolfe Tones 2016 CD 006 Warfield Music

Compilations

50 Great Irish Rebel Songs…: 2005 Dolphin DWWT3CD1 CD Compilation as "Derek Warfield & The Wolfe Tones"

God Save Ireland: 2006 KELLS7147 CD — Compilation of all previously released songs

Videos

Legacy: 1995 Apllo APV 90 VHS

Compilation DVD

Beneath A Dublin Sky-The 1916 Easter Rising 2006- Dolphin Records updated: 13/7/2017

P.S. A happy time was had by all at Barrowlands 2017

Bibliography

www.wolfetonesofficialsite.com Brian Warfield articles
Ernie O'Malley On Another Man's Wound / Roberts Rinehart
Tom Barry Guerilla Days in Ireland / Anvil Books
Dan Breen My Fight for Irish Freedom / Anvil Books
Kieran Allen 1916: Ireland's Revolutionary Tradition / Pluto Press
Mary Corcoran & Mark O'Brien ed Political Censorship and
Democracy / The HC State: The Irish Braodcasting Ban Four Courts
Press
Charlotte Despard: A Biography. Margaret Mulvihill / Pandora
Gerard O hAllmhurain Irish Traditional Music / the O'Brien Press
Dorothy Mcardle ed The Tragedies of Kerry 1922-1923. 17th edition /
Emton Press
Fiona Slevin By Hereditary Virtues – a history of Lough Rinn /
Coolabawn Publishing
Raymond Daly & Derek Warfield Celtic & Ireland in Song and Story
/ Amazon
 Bion Experiences in Groups / Routledge
Kevin Meagher A United Ireland -Why unification is inevitable and
how it will come about / Blackrock Publishing
Modelling Irish Unification. KLC Consulting Vancouver BC Canada
MacLeod, Alan Stuart (2012) The United Kingdom, Republic of
Ireland,United States and the conflict in Northern Ireland, August
1971 -September 1974. PhD thesis. Glasgow University

http://hudoc.echr.coe.int/eng?i=001-893 Application No.15404/89 by
Betty PURCELL et al against Ireland decision: 16/4/1991
Crotty v An Taoiseach   Legal references: [1987] IESC 4 (9 April 1987)
[1987] IESC 4, [1987] IR 713, [1987] ILRM 400, [1987] 2 CMLR
666, (1987) 93 ILR 480.
Purcell Betty Inside RTE a memoir / New Island
Hayden Talbot Michael Collins' Own Story / Edmund Burke:
Publisher
www.irish-folk-songs.com
www.irish-showbands.com
www.enjoy-irish-culture.com
www.independent.ie
www.irishcentral.com
www.wikipedia.com
www.historyireland.com
www.bbc.co.uk/history
www.rte.ie Insurrection. - docu drama 2016 [first shown1966]

www.theballadeer.com
www.irishtimes.com
www.limerickcity.ie
www.amazon.com
www.esri.ie/publications/attitudes   Attitudes In The Republic Of
Ireland Relevant To The Northern Ireland Problem: Vol.1 Descriptive
1/1/1979 General Research Series
www.wcml.org.uk
www.cain.ulst.ac.uk/issues/policy/docs   Breakthrough Northern
Ireland September 2010
www.irishrevolution.ie/irelands-songs-rebellion Marjorie Brennan

http://www.ireland-information.com
www.enjoy-irish-culture.com
Breakthrough Northern Ireland

The Economist Jan 22nd 2015| BELFAST
 takelessons.com April 24
2014http://www.bbc.com/future/story/20170823-the-channel-tunnel-
that-never-was-built

https://primephonic.com/news-pitched-the-sound-of-classical-music-
in-the-football-stadium

They do smile (Dwyer McClorey)

About the Author

Alex Fell is a sociology honors graduate, a former senior forensic psychiatric social worker and human rights lawyer. With a love of music from her family background as the daughter and great granddaughter of prominent musicians, and personal experience, she has a strong sense of justice. The Wolfe Tones' story reeks of injustice. This is her third book.

In addition to her second commissioned book the Complete Book of In Hand Showing, she wrote the ground breaking first book ever on The Irish Draught Horse which collated oral history and pedigree information in the nick of time from the old men who kept the breed alive in the teeth of the destructive policies of, in that case, the Department of Agriculture, interviewing, finding lost records and compiling pedigree charts. It is relevant to this work because Ireland's only native breed of horse was greatly affected by the Penal Law as was Irish folk music. It is also an international star as are the Wolfe Tones and both are worthy of immense national pride.

Irishness is something She took for granted, only very recently discovering the achievements of Charlotte Despard the suffragette, a distant relative. She too had cared about Irish injustice only in the early 20th century when, helped by her friend Maud Gonne, she morally and financially supported strikers and prisoners' families. The strange thing is that Charlotte Despard's brother, as Field Marshal French, was instrumental in recognising and registering the Irish Draught Horse, discovered also after that book was written. A link to Irish music too in the form of another remote relative Percy French a writer of music hall songs. Researching this book finally explained why her grandfather chose to call his son Parnell.